S0-BIZ-387

" . . . style, substance, and versatility."

Ellery Queen's Mystery Magazine

Praise for JOHN C. BOLAND's novels

"Roars along like a BMW in heat."

Kirkus Reviews on DEATH IN JERUSALEM

"Entertaining whodunit. Great fun!"

USA Today on EASY MONEY

"A wry insider's view of stock fraud, corporate raiders, genteel brokerage houses, and Wall Street ethics. . . . Breathtakingly plausible, both in its Wall Street manipulations and in its emotional center. Trenchant, sly—and cerebral fun throughout."

Kirkus Reviews on EASY MONEY

"Hang on around the corners!"

Washington Times on DEATH IN JERUSALEM

"It's the bulls, the bears and, above all, the sharks as John Boland takes us backstage at the stock exchange. Clean-cut, verb-packed sentences . . . reminding us that in the category of mean streets, Wall is up there."

Philadelphia Inquirer on EASY MONEY

"A breezy tale of financial intrigue."

Baltimore Sun on BROKERED DEATH

"Deftly entertaining."   *Easton Star Democrat on THE MARGIN*

Also look for **30 YEARS IN THE PULPS** *by* JOHN C. BOLAND

PerfectCrimeBooks.com

"A fast-paced story. . . . Nice plot swerves."

Baltimore Sun on EASY MONEY

"[A] wry, intelligent Wall Street mystery."

Publishers Weekly on DEATH IN JERUSALEM

"Very much in the Dick Francis tradition."

Ellery Queen's on EASY MONEY

"The Welles' prickly marital relationship is an element that adds substance to *The Margin*. Character development is not a strong suit in mysteries, but Anne, through forging a strong bond with [the villain's] 11-year-old daughter, begins to break out of her shell. *The Margin* is also distinguished by Boland's skill at keeping several plots going at once. . . . In all instances, lives are seriously threatened."

Arizona Daily Star on THE MARGIN

"Boland, who thinks like Paul Erdman and writes like Dick Francis, creates a winsome hero in Welles—and again scores big with this tale of complicated money maneuvering and family strife."

Kirkus Reviews on RICH MAN'S BLOOD

"Intriguing. . . quite readable. He excels in rendering epiphanies and, more impressively, in the painstaking creation of a sympathetic character from a dense tangle of inner conflicts."

Publishers Weekly on RICH MAN'S BLOOD

"Propels the reader straight into the world of high finance, low finaglings, terrorism and double dealings, all played out with consummate skill."

Baltimore Jewish Times on DEATH IN JERUSALEM

LAST ISLAND

SOUTH

Books *by* JOHN C. BOLAND

Novels

Last Island South   (2009)
The Margin   (1995)
Death in Jerusalem   (1994)
Rich Man's Blood   (1993)
The Seventh Bearer   (1993)
Brokered Death   (1992)
Easy Money   (1991)

Short Stories

30 Years in the Pulps   (2009)

Nonfiction

Wall Street's Insiders   (1985)

LAST ISLAND

SOUTH

JOHN C. BOLAND

Perfect Crime

Baltimore

LAST ISLAND SOUTH. Copyright © 2009 by John C. Boland. All rights reserved. No part of this book may be reproduced, transmitted or stored by any means without written permission except in the case of brief quotations embodied in critical articles or reviews. For information, address Perfect Crime, P.O. Box 26228, Baltimore, MD 21210. Email: PerfectCrime@att.net.

Visit: www.PerfectCrimeBooks.com

Part of this novel appeared, in substantially different form, under the title "Last Island South" in *Ellery Queen's Mystery Magazine* September/ October 2008.

Printed in the United States of America.

Cover photo: © 2009 JupiterImages Corp. All rights reserved. Used by permission.

This book is a work of fiction. The events and characters described herein are imaginary and are not intended to refer to actual places or living persons.

Library of Congress Cataloging-in-Publication Data
Boland, John C.
Last Island South / John C. Boland.
ISBN: 978-0-982-51578-5

First Edition: September 2009
10 9 8 7 6 5 4 3 2 1

For Alex and Martha

1

Don't tell me about sunny Key West.

First day of a bright New Year, rain slashing my father's boat, which was ten meters of rot and old varnish that leaked in the head and the galley and, more ominously, below the water line. I was wearing wool socks, sweat pants and a hooded jacket and my toes were cold anyway. The lowest temperature ever recorded in Key West was 46 degrees, and we had come close overnight. The boat's only heater was on the fritz. I was chugging down my second pot of green tea as I listened to my visitor.

"You got a reputation as a bad girl," Hub Bennell said. "Was it drugs?"

"Not lately."

"You're not as dumb as some ex-cops I could

name." He grinned to show he meant no harm, a big, middle-aged Conch, filling half my galley in his yellow slicker, sun scabs on the nose and the thickened hands of someone who had done real work before becoming a politico. He had served seven or eight years on the city commission without getting indicted, which was close to a record. After the last municipal scandal over hack licenses, Commissioner Hub Bennell told a TV reporter that he was sure he wasn't any more honest than the two commissioners who'd been arrested, so he guessed he was just slower to spot an opportunity. He said it with a melancholy, up-from-under grin that meant, *Dang if it ain't sad what goes on here.* A town where city notables used to import marijuana loves winks and nods.

If I wanted to, I could blame my father for the pinkety-plink of rain hitting the pan on the alcohol stove. He could have found time to do some maintenance. But I couldn't blame him for Hub Bennell. When Hub phoned, claiming a fleeting saloon acquaintance with Dad, I could have told him to get lost.

"I'd rather deal with smart than good any day," Hub assured me. Without invitation, he took down a mug from a railed shelf and poured hot water on instant coffee.

"This is the way I wish I lived," he said, nodding to the cabin. "Simple and honest."

"You want to live where the roof leaks."

"I told your dad the same thing I'm telling you. He had a good life here."

My father's life had been neither simple nor honest, if Hub wanted to pretend those were his standards, but he had stayed in town long enough that people thought they knew him.

"Did he borrow money from you?" I asked.

"No, honey, I'm sure he didn't. Let me tell you about my little problem. Shem said your cop friend lets you do security work. Shem said you stayed sober. That's Shem the Tailor."

I nodded. Shem the Tailor, who sold video games.

"You know I got this business—we fly tourists out to the Tortugas for sightseeing? Got me two Cessnas, two pilots. We hangar the planes about a mile from here. I need a night watchman, or – woman. There's thirty, forty thousand in engine parts and electronics I don't want ripped off. So can you help me out?"

"I'll be glad to. When do you need me?"

"Tonight. Maybe tomorrow, too."

"Have you seen prowlers?"

"Just had some footprints and tire tracks. Figure first trip they were casing the hangar. Maybe tonight they come with a truck."

I thought of suggesting he'd just had a visit from a midnight drunk looking for a plane ride. But I couldn't afford to talk myself out of a job.

He frowned as if he'd just thought of something. "Listen, maybe I need a big firm for this. Get someone to cover the hangar *and* my house."

"You have engine parts at your house?"

He planted a red-fingered hand on the ceiling. "Got guns and stuff I don't want walking off. It occurs to me, if I was settin' up a burglary, I'd see if the guy was at work before hitting his house. I got an alarm system at home, but by the time those county cops respond, the place could be empty." He squinted at me. "You like guns?"

"Not much."

"Your dad said he taught you to shoot."

I changed the subject. "I can hire a helper," I said. I knew a couple people who wouldn't take naps on the job. I had been doing low-rent security gigs for about three months, after finding I wasn't temperamentally suited to having my butt grabbed in a saloon.

We worked out a schedule. He told me again I had it made. Too bad about my daddy. Pocketing a check written on Bennell's Air Charter, I watched him lope across the marina yard to a small green convertible. The rain was still coming sideways. Two sea gulls and a pelican shared a bench outside the marina office, heads tucked, backs turned to the weather, feathers rippling. There are several popular nicknames for Key West—Conch Republic; when the sun's out, Paradise. But I think of it as Key Wasted.

While the tea kettle rattled, I straightened up the boat that was the main part of my inheritance. For my father the *KeyHole* had represented both sanctuary and freedom. A man with a boat could remove himself from a place with too many emotional ties and find a port where the drinking flag went up at daybreak and never came down.

He had found the right place. I had come down four months ago to clear up his estate. That hadn't been much of a job, but I kept finding reasons not to leave.

2

Hawkes Marina was on the south side of the island. Two blocks east lay Bahama Village, where roosters crow at midnight. Nobody at the marina had had a boat broken into since October, possibly because our boats looked shabbier than the neighborhood's single-story houses, which were getting bid up in the real estate boom. I didn't bother locking the *KeyHole* before I walked across the road. Any self-respecting burglar visiting the boat would drop off canned goods.

The Carbuncle had survived the storm. Too bad, maybe. I paid for a soft drink at the bar, pulled a chair upright and sat at a table littered with pizza scraps and firecracker paper from the New Year celebration. Lem Rees, who was part owner, came over bearing a bowl of chili I hadn't asked for.

"You left early," he said. "Missed the biker strip-tease."

"I didn't see it," I corrected him. "That's not the same as missing it. What time did I leave?"

"You don't remember?" Lem showed me teeth that should have been in a mummy case. His gray-streaked hair hit his shoulders; his bloodshot eyes could have been traced with red liner. Jailhouse X's were tattooed on the backs of his fingers.

"I remember having to knee someone to get out the door," I said. "Was it you?"

"Maybe Francis. He was keeled over puking about two a.m." Lemuel scratched his chest, tracing slow circles. "So it wasn't the chili."

I put down the spoon. My stomach hadn't felt good to begin with. According to a sign over the bar, the Carbuncle's chili had simmered in the same pot since the night Nixon resigned. Lem Rees told female customers that he was living proof the chili could cure most STDs.

"When did you close up?" I said.

"Didn't. The party just moved on."

"Where?"

"Bunch of people went to Gloria's. A few others decided on Smathers Beach. If you're looking for your artist pal, I think he was with the first group."

"Thanks."

"Is he still bunking with you?"

It was none of Lem's business, and the way he was rubbing his fingertips across his chest was creepy.

He noticed me watching and winced.

"Gets cold like this, my nipples hurt," he said.

My artist friend Tim—known as Timbo around town but as Timothy Scott Wheeler to his parents and the handful of people who had bought his paintings— had not returned when I got back to the boat. His paint box and canvases were racked beside the fridge— everything a little neater than before I had straightened up—his clothes mostly in cupboards or his backpack, his Grundig radio on a railed bookshelf, the weed in a tea tin, minimal toiletries since he didn't shave and used my shampoo and deodorant, just over six weeks' evidence we were keeping house together. I had never supported a boyfriend before, and I found the responsibility funny. He didn't eat much, but the tab for beer and dope was part of the reason I was eager for Bennell's job. As soon as Tim sold a painting he planned to pay me back. In the meantime, I wondered where he had woken up.

Last night's party hadn't begun at Gloria Hutchin's. It hadn't, to be technical, begun last night but had been running for several days, as you would expect in a party town. Tim and I had picked up the celebration around six in the evening, just as the rain blew in. We had stopped at Gloria's for drinks, elaborately kissed off the bad old year that was ending, laid it out straight and stiff with solemn benedictions for the bastard it had been, and assigned extravagant promise to the year that was about to begin. A year of cold beer and hot men. I was ready.

Instead of phoning Gloria to see if Tim had washed up there, I walked a dozen blocks into the quieter part of Old Town where she had a house and a couple of guest cottages.

There was no sign of Gloria or her friends on the broad porch facing William Street. I stepped through a wooden arch to the back, out of the rain for a moment. Two tiny houses at the rear of her compound accommodated an array of permanent and floating freeloaders. The right side of the patio was sheltered by a sprawling banyan tree, which was surrounded by iron chairs and a loveseat. On the other side of the path was a long pool. I walked over to the apron. Gloria was swimming laps in the rain.

At the far end, she turned and saw me.

"Megan, dear!"

Paddling to the side, she leaned onto the apron. She had young, pretty eyes in a sun-crinkled face, but she wasn't young. Veins like tree roots curled across the backs of her hands. Her short hair was sunset-red, cinched to her skull. The day I inspected the *KeyHole*, Gloria had appeared at the dock and introduced herself. Gloria Hutchin, ex-CIA, ex-Bryn Mawr, ex-wife twice over, proud and true drinking buddy of Daniel Trevor. She said we had met when I was a kid. Since she remembered the kid as sweet and pretty, I accepted the story, invited her aboard the boat, told her she could have the damn thing because

I was only staying a week. Five months later, I was still planning to leave town.

"Join me," she said. "A swim will repair last night's damage."

"I didn't bring a suit."

"Pooh, none of my boys will mind a bare butt."

"I'm wet enough." The green cap with the big swordfish bill hadn't even kept my face dry. My jacket was soaked through. "I'm looking for Tim."

"Mislaid him?"

I smiled, played along. "Is that what he says?"

"You're naughty. Tim was with us earlier. My God but I lost track of things." She dragged a hand across her face. "Did I wish you a Happy New Year? I think we were at Blackbeards sometime after dawn, but I can't remember what came before that. People kept dropping off. When did you leave?"

"People tell me it was around two."

"No hangover?" She looked prepared to be indignant. "You don't look hung over. I thought Tim came back here. A few never-say-dies are passed out in the cottages. You can check. I kept the big house locked. Too goddamn much stuff disappears when I'm trusting."

"I'll look in the cottages."

"I hope my boys didn't have their way with your fella. He would be ruined for mere woman."

"I guess I'd better go and find out."

"I'm sure it's all right." She reached a wet arm, across the bricks, beckoning me. "This will be a good year for you, Megan. No more sorrows. All right?"

"Sounds great," I said.

"It's what your father would wish."

I nodded. It was close to what he would say, too. Don't waste yourself on it—deliberately vague about "it," but grief was certainly on his list of things to be avoided. Grief, regret, responsibility.

"Leave the sorrows to me," she said. "I enjoyed Dan's company. We had clawed our way over some of the same ground. The bastards gang-raped me on the Isle of Pines. Your father was tortured there. It was all a very long time ago."

They must have had a great time as he knocked back her gin, reminiscing about Playa Giron and the Mosquito Coast, picking at wounds that never healed.

I went searching for a hung-over artist.

A man was standing by stove in the smaller cottage, jabbing a spatula at a smoking pan of eggs. He lifted an eyebrow. "Is Gloria awake?"

"In the pool." I heard voices from the next room. "I'm looking for my boyfriend, blond, beard, ponytail, answers to—"

"Am I to be the only cook?"

I went through the doorway. People were sprawled on cushions on the floor, three guys, one girl though she was well past girlhood, probably thirty, with a narrow freckled face and long-plaited hair that swung between her shoulders like a lash as she talked with

Tim, missing Tim, who leaned into her words, elbows on his knees. He didn't look damaged by the night of celebration. His face was pale, but since he couldn't tolerate much sun his face was always pale. With his gingery beard, he was one of the few guys I didn't think looked absurd with a ponytail. He wore blue jeans and sandals, no socks, a multi-striped shirt with the tails out.

He looked up. "Hey Meggie, where'd you get to?" He spoke as if I'd been there a minute ago.

The girl-woman craned her neck to see me.

"This is Grace," Tim said. "These are Kevin and"— he looked at a small man with a handlebar mustache —"I forget."

"Me, too," said the mustached man. "Amnesia's going to be the order of the day. Grace-love is telling us about Belize. She lived there last year working on a song cycle."

"Completing it," Grace said. "I insist on completing things I start." By her tone, there was no room for levity when it came to getting things done. She was sitting cross-legged, wearing some kind of homespun dress and sandals. Her skin was uniformly honey colored. She had several beaded bracelets on each wrist. Stretching out her arms for balance, she rose smoothly, using leg power alone, and announced she was going to take a shower.

"The main thing, from an artist's perspective, is the cost of living," said Kevin. His left eye rolled sideways. There were deep creases on his forehead.

"It's dirt cheap to live in Belize. Also there is a fair measure of personal freedom—not enough cops to bother us most of the time. We had neighbors who grew a little pot and nobody hassled them. Tim, you're having trouble selling your paintings, hunh?"

"Yeah."

"Belize is the place for this boy," said the man with the mustache. "Kevin and Grace-love are going back to the rain forest." He cast a glance at me. "Perhaps your friend could accompany them?"

"To Belize?" I said.

"Cheap living, creative space."

They had been discussing this before I arrived. I was an intruder, standing as the others sat, Kevin flicking glances between my boyfriend and Handlebar, who wore a clever smile.

"You're already living cheap," I told Tim.

He managed to look embarrassed. Moving aboard, he had been sorry he was tapped out and couldn't help with the slip fees. Felt guilty freeloading. Arrangement wasn't fair to me, etc.

"This could be a chance for me to do some really edgy work, Meggie. Rainforest stuff. Maybe a gallery would take it."

"Can't stifle an artist," said Handlebar.

"I haven't been much of an artist," Tim said, talking to the others. "Her father croaked, you see, and left her this crappy boat. It barely floats, and we're on top of each other all the time. Can't get anything done."

Handlebar nodded understanding.

Being on top of each other, I thought crudely, had been part of the attraction six weeks ago.

For a moment, wondering if money was the problem, I was tempted to tell Tim not to worry about expenses, I really didn't mind. But I didn't say anything. People who sleep together get a little psychic, but I didn't need that channel to feel pretty sure he had decided to go. He didn't have the nerve to say it, so he was letting his new friends say it for him. I wondered how he would pay for an air ticket to South America.

"'Chick with boat'," said Handlebar. "That would be a good line in the classifieds, love, to get yourself a new roomie." He was watching me, hoping for a reaction. I thought about kicking him.

Tim and I had never implied commitment. It had been a hookup, maybe a little more than that but not much. He'd had his French easel out on Mallory Square, and I had admired a sketch. We had split a pizza while he told me why the sketch was crap. Sooner or later, one of us would move on.

Kevin was businesslike. "Grace and I can help Tim get his stuff off your boat."

Just like that.

"I figured you would be okay with this, Meggie," Tim said. His tone implied he would be disappointed if I was surly and immature.

"If it's what you want," I said.

The day seemed a little emptier than it should have. But not too empty.

Let the rain forest have him.

3

I'm not the most experienced private security person in the Florida Keys, just one of the cheapest. A guy with Hubbard Bennell's connections could afford to go first class, so I was pleased he had hired me to do the watchman gig. The rain had stopped at dusk and the wind had settled down. Bottom-lighted clouds scudded over Old Town like ships setting out across the windy dark miles to the Everglades. The windshield of Babe McKenzie's pickup truck was opaque with mist, but I was doing my surveillance with the driver's side mirror, which I wiped every few minutes with fingers that weren't holding the Thermos cup of tea. I had a plastic salad container on the passenger's seat, empty except for vinegar and a fork. Behind me the air charter yard was closed, office lights out, airplane hangar locked and dark. The hangar was actually a converted boathouse sitting at the edge of the lagoon that Bennell's two planes used for takeoffs and landings. Most of his customers were tourists who wanted to make day trips to Fort Jefferson, which lay seventy miles out onto the Gulf of Mexico in a tiny island cluster called the Dry Tortugas. Both of Bennell's high-winged Cessnas were fitted for water landings.

I had babysat Hub for an hour at his office, and he seemed to welcome the company. Now it was eleven-thirty, he had gone home hours ago, and no one had come around to steal engine parts. I'd driven away twice for a few minutes, trying to lure somebody out of the brush, but it hadn't worked.

I punched the number of Babe McKenzie's phone. She was supposed to be watching my client's house.

"Any action?"

"Nothing. What did you expect?"

"Have you made the rounds?"

She had a friendly streak, and if nobody checked on her she might sit in the kitchen drinking beer with Hub and bullshitting. She dressed like someone on the Dick Clark re-runs that my mom watched. She was a few years past fifty, with smoke-cured skin, electric blond hair, and about twice as much chest as you would expect on a five-two frame. Hub Bennell hadn't taken his eyes off her nubby white sweater.

"I been around the place three times," Babe said. "Right now it's pretty cold on the deck and I gotta pee."

I wiped the mirror. Something had moved. A pint-sized keys raccoon was making its way to the water. I didn't expect other visitors. Anyone wanting something from Bennell's office or the hangar could have torn the place apart when nobody was watching. Having walked the property in the twilight, I hadn't found much of a trove of spare parts in the hangar. Not much to interest a prowler.

Which made the job stink a little. And here I was, someone with a dubious personal reputation, never mind the family history, staking out a little place where a plane could land in the dark. The first thing you think about is drugs coming in. The second is people.

"I'm heading over your way," I told Babe. "Hold the bathroom break till I get there."

"You better drive fast," she said.

Bennell's house stood on pilings beside a canal out near the Gulf Breeze condominiums. He had the usual wraparound deck, a lattice-enclosed storage area at ground level, and parking spaces behind the house. I pulled Babe's truck up behind the client's BMW. From the deck, Babe waved at me.

"Couldn't wait for the potty break, honey. Want me to toss you a beer?"

"Where's Bennell?"

"Inside watching a show about horny doctors. You ought to know something. He's got a gun under the couch. I saw it sticking out. Could be a forty-five."

I climbed up to the deck. Half of Florida keeps guns under the couch or in the glove compartment of a car. It's the half that causes trouble, or expects it.

Babe tipped her beer and looked north, but there was nothing much to see. Gulf Breeze was a quarter mile past us, four mid-rise buildings hugging the water and painting the sky lavender, though it could have been green given the money living out there. The nearest stilted house along the access road was three hundred yards back toward the highway. The only traffic I'd seen since the turnoff was a Lexus beating home to the condos.

"He's a tidy guy for a bachelor," said Babe. Her mind was drifting. She had two cats to support. Bennell had a little money. If we got another night on the job, she would show up in spike heels and a cocktail dress. Tonight she had on running shoes—I'd had to convince her cowboy boots were for dancing—snug jeans and a denim jacket over the sweater. Somewhere in the jacket she had an airweight thirty-eight and one or two speedloaders. She'd had a life up north as a sheriff's deputy or a hooker, depending how she wanted to tell it.

She got close and said, "How much do you think that fatty's worth?"

"I don't know."

"You think he likes cats?"

"Ask him."

"If I say it wrong, I sound like a whore. Great deck, ain't it? Imagine sitting out here at sunset with a maitai and a slab of ribs. Waving at boaters passing off the point. Maybe flippin' off the ones in little tubs."

"That could be me in one of the little tubs."

"You never leave the dock."

I rapped at the sliders, and the TV went off and he opened a door.

"Nothing doing at the hangar," I said, stepping past him. "I need to use the loo."

He pointed and I went round a couple of corners. Bypassing the green-tiled bathroom, I followed the hall to a bedroom where the lights were on. Babe hadn't mentioned the shotgun lying atop a wicker chest of drawers. It was a scratched-up side-by-side, with the safety on, as if anyone could trust a safety on a twelve gauge. Feeling superstitious, I pulled a few tissues from a box at the bedside and made certain I left no fingerprints on the gun as I broke it open. The shells were double-ought, which put the ideal game pretty high up the evolutionary ladder.

I flushed the tissues down the toilet, came back and made a quick tour of the kitchen and a side room, which he'd fixed up as a den with a gun case on one wall. There were two rifles in the locked case and a shotgun with decorative engraving, probably worth some money. I don't know how many weapons a middle-aged guy in Florida needs to qualify as a gun nut, but I guessed he wasn't close to the number. There were plaques on the wall honoring Hubbard Bennell for this and that. A dozen photos hanging in two rows showed Hub with people who must have been important. If you knew the faces, which I didn't, the display probably added up to a local civics lesson. I returned to the living room, which was empty, and took a minute to look around. The handgun that Babe had mentioned wasn't under the sofa or its flowery cushions, which made me think Bennell might have the gun inside the big loose shirt he was wearing as he hunched on the deck, elbows on the railing, soft-talking Babe.

He didn't seem worried that I'd left his engine parts unguarded, so I guessed I didn't have to be.

I went outside. Farther up the canal, I saw a couple of lights glimmering through a sparse line of trees. There were still patches of old Florida out here, away from the highway, full of poisonwood and arma-dillo and methamphetamine, along with crazy people who went fishing every day and sane people hiding from the world.

"I'll go back to the hangar," I told Bennell, "but I don't think anyone's staking out the place."

His grin was as white as cracked lobster. My going back to the charter yard was a great idea, and he'd just hang on the deck with Babe.

When Bennell went to get another beer, I told her, "There's a shotgun in the bedroom loaded with double-ought."

"He joked about the handgun."

"Joked?"

"Said the palmetto bugs was getting big and feisty."

"Cute."

"Yeah, he sure is that." Digging into her jacket, she pulled out a snub-nosed revolver with a recessed hammer, swung the cylinder out, then closed it making sure the empty chamber was under the hammer. One reason I liked working with Babe was she was reasonably sensible about guns. In Florida any resident who isn't officially insane or a criminal can be issued a permit to carry a concealed weapon. That fact makes me a very polite driver. As far as Babe would admit, she had never shot anyone up north or down here.

"What do you make of this job?" I asked. "There's nothing at the charter yard worth stealing, and the gun collection isn't so hot."

"Is this the first time a guy lied to you, honey?"

We went downstairs, walked around the brick patio that bordered the canal. Bennell came out and watched his hired girls. We set off in opposite directions, walking to the edge of the property where skunk cabbage and snakes tangled in the dark. I went around to the road and heard feet swishing through weeds as she came the other way. The blond hair was visible first, like a ball of electricity floating five feet above the ground. As she drew close, she said, "Look, if he had anything real bad going on, he'd hire bigger guns."

"Maybe he's too cheap."

"You're gonna make me nervous yet."

I nodded. I moved away, to look at the other end of the house. Nobody was hiding there, at least nobody

I could see.

"Maybe Hubbard has screwed someone's wife," Babe called. "For a fattie, he *is* cute."

"A hunk," I said, heading to her truck. "I'm going back to the airplanes."

I wondered if Tim had gotten his stuff off my boat.

4

The shots came from the canal side of the house. *Pok-pok.*

Then a string of small *pak-pak-pak-paks* like fire-crackers on a wet night. Fifty feet away, Babe was frozen in mid-step except for her head, which swerved from the sound to me. Sensible people do not run toward gunfire. They stand and shiver, and I was glad to see we were both sensible people. She had pulled her gun and had it pointed a few feet in front of her, not at the sky like girl detectives do on TV as they run with their lungs bouncing and their pinkie fingers extended. She didn't run at all.

Five seconds passed without another sound. No-body was shooting. Nobody was screaming.

The poks had been the heavier loads, presumably

driving larger slugs.

"Shit," said Babe. She could see herself supporting the cats into old age.

I gave it another fifteen seconds, then left the truck and went around the house. Nobody was on the patio beside the canal, nor on the elevated wooden deck as far as I could see. There was a lot of deck where someone could be lying flat and I wouldn't know it. Out on the water an outboard motor was moving away. The sound made me think of my favorite kid's movie, which had a dragonfly named Evinrude who powered the rescuers' leaf boat through the bayous. The buzzing on the canal wasn't much louder than a movie dragonfly's. It was already pretty far away.

I stood at the bottom of the stairs, off to the side where I could move under the deck in a hurry.

"Mr. Bennell!"

No answer. Climbing up to where a possibly wounded man hugged a twelve gauge shotgun wouldn't be smart. Even if he just had the .45, going up was dumbsville.

"Bennell!"

"Hope he's playing possum," Babe McKenzie said. She was somewhere behind me. I didn't look around. I was listening to the noises that had replaced gunfire and the boat's motor. There was a little wet *slip-slip* against the bulkhead from the boat's wake. On both sides of us birds were complaining about the way the neighborhood had gone to hell.

I took a step, crunched on a shell casing, let it lie.

Hub Bennell cleared his throat overhead. "Some excitement, huh?" His voice wobbled. I went up the stairs to the deck. He was pale and trembling, trying to maintain a grin, his hand touching the butt of a pistol in his front pocket, the way someone touches a wallet with too much money in it. The shots from the boat had scattered glass across the floor of his living room. He'd switched off the lights sometime during the festivities and hadn't put most of them back on.

"Was this the burglar you were expecting?" I said.

"Not exactly."

When my phone came out, his big eyes popped. "Who are you calling?"

"Cops."

"I don't think I hit anybody."

"That's good. Also, legally speaking, beside the point. Who was in the boat?"

"There was two of 'em. When I saw the one son of a bitch had a gun, I was too busy duckin' to see much else."

I switched on the patio flood lights and went down to the canal. There was nothing on the bricks that looked like blood. That didn't mean he hadn't hit anyone.

Bennell said from the deck, "See, nobody hurt."

"So you tell the police that."

Climbing the stairs, I had the phone out again. Instead of talking to him, I should have been calling.

"We bring the police in, it's gonna mess me up," he said.

"How does it mess you up? Are your guns legal?"

"Guns are fine." He saw my fingers weren't tapping buttons. "Come on inside."

I stepped over the glass.

His drinking was informal. Instead of having a picklewood bar in a corner of the living room, he kept his bottles in the kitchen next to the microwave. He poured bourbon for himself. Babe took another beer. I shook my head. Bennell propped himself against the refrigerator. "Remember Cole Yates?"

"No."

"He was mayor."

"The one that ran away," Babe supplied.

"Okay." I remembered vaguely. Cole Yates had been barroom talk when I hit town: real estate developer turned mayor turned fugitive. Maybe he hadn't needed to run, because whatever was being investigated hadn't led to an indictment. So he became an object of fun. Wonder if the mayor knows it's okay to come home? Wonder if Mrs. Yates is gettin' serviced? High-toned stuff like that. TV pictures had shown him with dark hair combed down on his forehead, wearing a look of ambitious sincerity. Not much else had stayed in my memory.

"What's this got to do with Yates?"

Bennell lowered his drink. "Feds were sniffing the mayor. When he disappeared, they turned on me, gave me a rough time. He was mayor, old Hub's on the City Commission. For them, that's enough to put us in bed together." His bottom lip drooped from yellowed teeth, loose and goofy.

Babe took a pull at a bottle of Key West Lager.

There had to be more. "And tonight?"

"I think somebody's got the idea I got a piece of whatever Cole's action was, so they'll squeeze me."

"Who?"

"No idea."

"What?"

"Gotta be money, don't it?"

"Do you?"

"No. Cole and me didn't go sharesy. If he stole anything, he kept it. Not that I think he did. Just the same, if the cops get involved tonight, everyone's going to start talking again. Maybe the feds'll get a renewed itch to persecute someone, that could be me."

"So why—" I stopped.

Babe leaned her head close to Bennell's. "That's okay, honey."

For about a second he thought her sweet tone meant he was getting sympathy.

"Me personally," she said, "I like having people shoot guns around me without knowing why. But Meggie looks pissed, don't she? She's probably gonna go ahead and call the cops."

He snuck a hurt look at me, then told her, "I didn't know there'd be shooting."

"Course you didn't, honey. But you were ready for it. Even fired the first shots, didn't ya?"

"The guy with the gun, I figured a couple shots

would scare him off."

"The lights were on down there," I said. "You must have seen him. What did he look like?"

"Younger than me, tall, kinda in shape. I only had a second."

Babe and I held a little conversation with our eyes. I think we sort of reached the same conclusion. Bennell might or might not know who was shaking him down. But tonight he'd planned to bushwhack them, with at least one of us as backup.

Babe was right. I was pissed. Pissed and ready to throw Hub to the first cop who answered the phone. If I didn't do that, I could still ditch the stupid job.

"Look," he said. . . .

Now he wanted to talk.

Eight nights ago, good warm evening. Hubbard Bennell has no family but he has buddies, the "Orphans," they call themselves, who get together around holidays so nobody gets lonely or suicidal. There were five of them this year. No presents, that was too much like a family holiday. Drinks and pricey dinner at Louie's, with the Atlantic rubbing the stone bulkhead along the restaurant's famous back yard, that was Christmas Eve, then a fishing trip to the Marquesas early the next morning on a boat Bennell owned. Not a single one of them melancholy even after the first case of beer is distributed on the bottom of the Gulf. Three of the Orphans are divorced, so they phone their exes or kids from the middle of nowhere, hear about whiteout in Buffalo or Chicago and decide their own lives are just fine, better than fine. The sky and sea are glassy reflections of their good mood.

One of them ribs Hub about the runaway mayor, gone five months now, how Hub must have had a piece of the Yates action, and on top of that how about a piece of Mrs. Yates's action, ugly old bastard that you are, Hub. He wouldn't mind a piece of either, he concedes, as money and pussy make the world go round, shaking his head in regret that he hasn't had more of both.

He is thinking of Yates four nights later.

He doesn't know what Cole Yates was into but can't help running ideas through his head. Most of them he dismisses as pretty dumb. Like helping Marielitos import drugs. In this little corner of Florida, it is no longer a low-risk, high-return business. It's a game for numbnuts. Yates isn't dumb enough. City treasury hasn't been tapped. No little boys have come forward saying the mayor was into their pants. And it had to be something big, anyway, to get all that federal attention.

So Cole Yates is on Hub's mind this cooling evening, December 29, when the phone rings and he hears a whispering man pretending to be Yates. Hub is actually deceived for ten or fifteen seconds.

"Did he sound like anyone else you know?" I said.

"He sounded like Cole, just not enough. He says I screwed him over and he's going to send someone. It was crazy, because I hadn't done any business with the mayor except the normal kind. Then I listen closer and I figure it isn't Cole, just someone doing a good imitation. Someone who's maybe heard something and figures he knows things he don't."

"Maybe he wants to scare you," Babe said. "Hopes you'll go check the hidey hole where you got the loot stashed."

"There ain't no loot."

"Who doesn't like you?" I said.

"Aw, c'mon, Meggie. Pretty much everyone likes me. Not that I'm a saint, but I get along with people. I don't go greedy on them." He stopped as though he'd just had a thought. "There's plenty enough down here to go around. I got more money if you and Miss Babe want to keep an eye on me a few days. I promise you, you know the worst."

He got sore an hour later when I wouldn't let him keep the shotgun in his bedroom. Ten minutes after that, calmed by a third of a bottle of bourbon, he was snoring. Babe had gone home to feed her cats and grab a few hours' sleep. We agreed on twelve-hour shifts. If the job stretched more than two days I would hire a third person. With all the lights off, I opened the drapes. As the cool air crept in through the broken glass I kept an eye on the canal.

Half my attention was on listening. The birds were back asleep. There were no sirens whooping in the distance, so I concluded that nobody had pinpointed the sound of the shots.

Why should I bother cops who had their hands full with other things.

Babe McKenzie relieved me at half-past eight, and I drove my client's BMW home to the boat. My boy-friend was gone. His paint box, his radio, his dope. He hadn't left a note.

5

My favorite police sergeant, Barry Irvington, was dressing down a beefy young cop for having man-handled a college student. The inundating wave of spring breakers wouldn't arrive until March, Barry pointed out, so it set a bad precedent to get the city sued in January. He leaned backward against his desk, arms folded across a hollow chest, the over-head fluorescents turning his scalp blue under a thin screen of blond hair. I had known him five months. He had called my mother in Connecticut with the bad news, then befriended me when I came down to dis-pose of the boat. The young cop, who had a stiff brown crewcut and a button nose, was paying grudg-ing attention.

"The kid you beat up could have a professor back

in Boston who is a constitutional lawyer. Would you like me to spell constitutional in dollars and cents?"

"He spit on me," protested the cop, who wasn't long out of school himself, though not out of a Boston law school. "He'd got thrown out of Margaritaville and—"

Barry waved for him to be quiet. "Okay, Terrence. Break their skulls." His head turned slightly. "Did you let her in the door?"

The young cop looked over his shoulder, tried to decide whether the sergeant wanted me thrown out or merely headlocked. While he wrestled with that, I slipped past him to a neutral corner.

"We have a problem," Barry said. "In eight weeks, the town will be overrun by several thousand drunken teenagers plus a few hundred bikers. Terrence, who is in his seventh month with the department, is ill-prepared. He identifies himself with the law. If he is offended, the law must be offended. If the law is offended, Terrence has a large hard fist."

Terrence's face was reddening all the way to the top of his head. He muttered, "I gotta get back on duty, if that's okay, sir," and huffed out of the office.

Watching him, Barry said, "They either get it or they don't. If they don't, they hurt someone."

"You never made a suspect eat pavement?" I asked. In three years of college, I had learned all about civil liberties and why I didn't like cops.

"Only the ones who deserved it. Terrence doesn't understand that distinction. He thinks they all deserve it." Pushing off his desk, he came over near me and then stopped abruptly, as if a peck on the cheek had been on his mind until he thought better of it. Having gotten me out of trouble, he didn't hide his pleasure in the fact I was earning a living instead of drinking. He said, "What do you want? Are you here on business?"

"I want to know about Mayor Yates. What happened, whether there was money left behind."

"Sounds like you've taken up treasure hunting."

Two weeks ago, a restaurant had hired me on Barry's recommendation to stop the theft of its premium liquor. My earnings for a few days of undercover work had paid three months of slip rental at the marina and bought me a cell phone. I had an obligation to be straight with Barry. I met it halfway.

"No treasure hunting," I said.

"So why do you care?"

"I got a security job. Sort of confidential. The name came up."

"I see. Well, you know Yates took off? He didn't have time to raise cash. Left behind an account with Merrill Lynch up in Miami, a small checking account at the Stock Island Bank, quite a bit of real estate."

"What was he running from?"

"You would have to ask the feds. There's been a joint task force of federal agencies operating down here for years, supposedly cooperating with local authorities. We didn't get let in on what they were doing on Yates. People from ATF and Customs kicked up dust for a few months, and then it got quiet."

"Could other city officials have been targets?"

"Nobody else left town. Nobody's been charged. Nothing was missing from city accounts."

"So there isn't any treasure to hunt."

"No sign of one."

"I heard he was married. What happened with Mrs. Yates?"

"She's still in town."

"Is she a suspect?"

"You mean, do we think she killed him? I wouldn't rule it out, but there's no evidence for it. When we talked to her, she gave all the right answers, didn't want a lawyer. I think—this was a few months ago—she expected him to come back. Or knew she'd hear from him, which she might have done."

"Did Yates have business partners?"

"Sure, a different partner for every dance."

"Any who would cheat him?"

"Every one of them, if the opportunity came about. Mostly Yates had pieces of other people's deals. And mostly he bought in with borrowed money. His wife has had to cut back."

The thought didn't seem to displease him. He said, "How's your painter friend?"

"Gone to Belize."

He nodded as if that were to be expected. "Come on, I'll buy you breakfast.,"

We had a good arrangement, from my perspective. He bought me a lot of breakfasts, didn't ask about dinners.

We went out the back door of the building, which doubles as City Hall and police headquarters, and he drove down to Duval.

Moses was on the corner of Fleming, swirling dingy robes and smoking a twenty-five cent stogie that he had packed with marijuana. The bearded man waved at us and winked as Barry drove through the intersection. Tourists loved Moses. Dropping out was an easy kind of performance art. Anyone could do it. Barry said, "His parents in Virginia send him a check every month so he'll stay in Florida."

There had to be a lot of such parents. Half the people in Key West had come from somewhere else, getting as far south as they could before they had to swim. Mom probably would have paid my father to stay away, if it had come to that.

The market had been slow, with too many fiberglass boats sitting at docks refusing to sink and no one to buy them. If I wanted to list the *KeyHole* with a broker, Larson & Larson were honest. They said they might move it in a year if the price was low. I decided to stay a few months in the place where so many people had known my father. I had spent a few summers here when he wasn't on assignment. I would see if a dozen drinks and a little dope sweetened the memories.

"Buy Tinker a rum," Barry had advised. Tinker was the fisherman who had found the *KeyHole* adrift. "He won't take a dime for towing your boat. Let him talk your leg off about Havana before the revolution. Let him tell you lies about himself and your father."

I had bought Tinker his rum, then made a mistake and bought him a few more and heard how just about for sure the Cubans had finally got Danny Trevor. Must have shot him and pushed the body overboard. Would have amputated this or that, too, because they did that sort of thing. If the mortal remains ever turned up, they wouldn't be pretty.

Tinker raising his glass, neither sad nor sober but wondering. Another rum, kid?

6

Bennell's Air Charter was out near Houseboat Row. Hub had an acre of scrubby land that looked worse in daylight than it had at night. He had landing rights on a ten-acre lagoon that was shaped like a stretched kidney. A high-winged plane with pink conch shells painted on the sides was taxiing across the shallow water toward the hangar. Beside the pilot in the cabin I could see a pale woman and in the back seat three small bobbing heads. I went into the boathouse and watched the plane dock. The woman wobbled out, holding onto the pilot's arm as if the ground was heaving. The kids spilled out and giggled at the woman's distress as she sank onto a bench near the door.

Noticing me, the pilot glanced at his watch. He was young and sunburned, good-looking if you can stand them clean-cut. His battered leather jacket and faded jeans looked as though they had been through a couple of wars the wearer had missed. If he was older than me, it wasn't by much.

"Are you part of the two o'clock?" he asked.

"No. I'm meeting Mr. Bennell."

He said "oh" and lost interest in me as he shook out a plastic bag and began clearing the cockpit of soda cans and a vomit cup.

A pint-sized Cuban man was holding down the office. He introduced himself as Luis and tried to sell me a sightseeing tour to the Dry Tortugas.

"It is beautiful sight, the old fortress, protecting nothing but empty water and pelicans."

"So I've heard."

"I could tell you the history. The fort was built before the Civil War. Your government has been spending money stupidly for a long time."

I'd heard that, too, but this time I said, "I don't like flying."

He leaned on the counter. "But you will go—one of these days, yes?"

He smiled, and I smiled, appreciating the joke. Everyone in Key West plans to make the seventy-mile trip to the islands one of these days. In the tropics, "one of these days" is a way of life. People who don't go somewhere their first weeks in town never go.

"I've been by boat," I told him, "years ago." Dad pointing into the shallows at the shimmering husks of planes and boats that had died making dope runs, telling me the right name for the Lower Keys should be the Contraband Republic.

When the pilot came in, he ignored me and said to Luis, "No sign of the boss yet?"

Luis shook his head.

The pilot dropped onto a rickety wooden chair. A plug of either tobacco or chewing gum filled one cheek. "I'm pumping the starboard float," he said. "It felt like we had a club foot taking off."

"They all leak," Luis told me, "but some leak worse. We say the same of engines. They all miss but some miss worse. If you want a tour, I personally will take you up in a one eighty-five that neither leaks nor misses. Steve is a bold pilot. I am an old pilot."

The younger man nodded. "Luis will be flying long after I've cracked up the last time."

He had noticed me after all and was trying to make flying sound glamorous. I gave him a schoolgirl smile. "Do you wreck a lot of planes, Steve, or just make your passengers airsick?"

He blew a large pink bubble. "Try for both."

I heard a car and went out as Bennell and Babe McKenzie arrived. They climbed out of her pickup truck. Hub was wearing a sheepish grin, and Babe was stretching her back. I decided I should hang out a shingle for Meggie's Protection and Escort Service. As long as Babe was willing and middle-aged guys couldn't resist that rack, we would do okay.

He came around the truck, hitching up his pants and sighing. "I got a business to run. Can't stay home hiding all the time."

We walked down to the boathouse, where a chattering pump was spitting dirty water.

"No more excitement?" I said.

"Been quiet. Maybe they gave it up."

"I think we scared them off," Babe said, letting me interpret that as I wished. She yawned and ambled back toward the cars.

"We can guard you," I told Hub. "But it would be better if we knew who we're dealing with. Tell me about your friends. Were any of them close to Yates?"

"You mean the Orphans? Nah, no way. Cole's friends like to figure they're on the way up. None of us would say that about ourselves."

"Describe them."

"Old guys, honey. The only newcomer is Chuck, been with us what—two years?—since his wife passed on. He pushes real estate, mostly winter rental stuff, down in the Truman Annex."

"Could any of the rentals belong to Yates?"

"How would I know? Cole did his stuff, I did mine. We didn't take showers together." It was the second or third time Hub had used a vaguely sexual reference in playing down his relationship with the mayor. I wondered if I should be paying closer attention. "Cole talked about us buying a boat together one time, something that would need work, but nothing came of it."

"Are any of your Orphans in the boat business?"

"Sure. Roger Pine and Johnny Slack both got a charter business just like me, except they make money. They're just over the bridge on Stock Island. Basic pontoon jobs, not too much capital invested."

"Which of them kidded you about having business dealings with Mayor Yates?"

"They all got an oar in before I got pissed and they stopped. Maurice started it. He asked if I'd been bonking Mrs. Yates. You seen her? Nice looking gal."

"Does Maurice know Mrs. Yates?"

"He knows everyone. Maurice Pohl. He's deputy police chief."

"Did any of the others take him seriously?"

"That I was doing Reena Yates?"

"That you had some of her husband's money."

His squint moved from the water pump to me. "Johnny Slack's dumb enough to believe it. But he wasn't on that boat last night."

"I thought you couldn't see clearly."

"Couldn't, but Johnny's fatter than me and the guys on the boat weren't fat."

"He could have sent them."

"No he couldn't've."

"Why not?"

"He don't need money, don't even care about it. He's sick and dying. Besides that, Johnny's been a friend of mine twenty-some years."

"What about Roger Pine?"

A loose smile formed. "He'd steal a scab off your

butt, but Rog knows me. If I'd been dealing with the mayor, I never could've kept my mouth shut. He was just kidding along with the others."

"Did any of the group miss New Year's Eve?"

"Nope."

"Did you tell them what was going on?"

"Nope."

We went back up the yard to his office, where he wrote down the phone numbers of his fellow Orphans. I hung around while Bennell did his paperwork, collected the morning's receipts, and ordered the two pilots to make extra careful preflight checks. Babe was napping in the Beemer's back seat when the two o'clock group of customers arrived. I went out and watched the club-footed plane with the pink conch shells painted on the side climb effortlessly off the lagoon, correct a few degrees, and shrink slowly in the bright sky toward the Tortugas.

7

My father swims behind the boat in the dying after-noon. The slate-colored Gulf lifts in low swells, from the top of which he can see the sunlit tip of a sail moving away from him. Each glimpse is briefer than the one before, and finally there is nothing but sky and water. No canvas wedge. No plunging birds. He is alone in a rolling gray desert. He swims down the backside of the swell . . . choking on sea water . . . losing the rhythm of his strokes. He doesn't sense the predatory shapes in the darkness, squirming toward the surface. . . .

Then I was awake and sweating, the warning I wanted to scream locked in my throat. A deaf neighbor's BBC report rattled cups across the marina. I got up and saw it was time to go to work.

It was dark when I set myself up outside the Yates house in Calusa Estates. I had Babe's truck, binoculars, an iPod to try to keep me awake. Each driveway cut between pretty little shell-encrusted gate posts topped with low-power lights. Coils of hemp decorated the tinted concrete walls, and Permastone dolphins stood on their tails balancing mail boxes. In certain stretches along the Overseas Highway, the dolphins would be painted in black face with exaggerated lips. These were just blue and cute.

Most of the cops who might drive past tonight would know that I didn't spot for burglary teams, but that didn't mean they would leave me alone. I didn't want to have to explain myself. Cops are bigger gossips than school girls, and it wouldn't help me if word reached Mrs. Yates that I had staked out her house.

After an hour of not seeing anything, I got out of the truck and looked up the driveway. The oceanfront house was partly visible. Lights were still on, but I wondered if anyone was home. The lights could be on timers. There wasn't a car in sight. I went over and opened the mailbox. There had been a mail delivery today, none yesterday, deliveries the two days prior to the holiday. I shined my penlight in. The box looked pretty full. She might have gone away. Or someone looking for Yates's money might have dropped by. In which case, Mrs. Yates could be lying in the nice house injured or dead. Sprawled on a patio, baking in the sun day after day.

I closed the mailbox, pulled out my phone and tried the Yates number. After a dozen rings, I gave up. I thought about calling the police, but the only thing I had to report was a full mailbox.

When I drove back to Bennell's and relieved Babe, she put an arm around my shoulders. "You know, honey, it's only a matter of time till people notice that Hubby Bear has protection. The police are going to have questions."

"Get some sleep."

"I left it your call, but we should have reported the shooting."

"I know. Go home."

"Don't want you to get in trouble, honey."

She had an annoying habit, which I tried to discourage, of making motherly noises around me. She probably thought in terms of being a big sister, which would put her in the age bracket she preferred: experienced but still perky.

This was our third time working together. On the last job, watching the city marina during a string of break-ins, she had warned me to stay away from sensitive guys because they turned out to be the biggest shits. I should have listened. No one claimed to be more sensitive than an artist. We had talked about forming a partnership to bid on bigger security jobs, but the idea hadn't gone anywhere. I wasn't going to push for it. By age and temperament, Babe would see herself as senior partner.

"What did Bennell tell the glass company?" I said. The big sliding doors had been replaced.

"He blamed a seagull. Must have been a flock of them, but nobody cared. I made sure there weren't any bullet holes or brass."

"Where are the shell casings?"

She handed me an envelope. "We can say we were preserving evidence."

"Go on home," I said. "I won't make any moves on Bennell."

"I'm not worried." She lifted a bleached eyebrow. "How are you and Tim doing?"

"He took off."

"I saw him a week or two ago hanging with a pair of dope fiends. Kevin and Grace, *artistes.*"

So it had been in the works for a while. As for Kevin and Grace's reputation, I shrugged. Who was I to talk? A few nights after learning my father was dead, I had thought mixing bourbon and mescaline was a good idea.

"One of those pilots was checking you out," she said.

"You were napping."

"I had an eye open. Pays to keep an eye open around cute guys. He was sizing up your butt."

"Go home," I said.

***

The day hadn't been a total write-off. I had talked with one of Hub's Orphans, the real estate broker. Thirty seconds after meeting Chuck Welsh at his office in the Truman Annex, I crossed him off my list. He was too timid to look up from his shoes more than once in the five minutes I was with him.

8

A couple of porpoises had swum a hundred yards up the canal. As I ate breakfast, leaning on the railing at the outermost corner of Hub Bennell's deck, they provided entertainment fifty feet off his seawall. There was none of the happy squeaking you hear in movies. They were quiet and purposeful. The only sound was the desperate thrashing at the surface as bait fish tried to climb out of the water to avoid the deft lunges that swallowed them.

On the bay, a tipsy sportfisher was headed for deep water, pulling a skein of pelicans above the wake. A busy, hungry morning.

I phoned Reena Yates's number twice. Not even a recorded message announced: *Milady is preparing for another day in the sun.* So maybe she was okay.

I waited until eight-fifteen to try Barry Irvington's pager. He called back and I told him about the over-stuffed mailbox and the unanswered telephone.

"Did you ring the doorbell?"

"No."

"Exactly why is this of concern to the police?" When I didn't answer right away, he said, "Do you have reason to believe Mrs. Yates needs help?"

"Not exactly."

"Why don't you come tell me about it." Despite the phrasing, it wasn't a question, or a suggestion. "I'm a few miles up the highway. There's something here you should see." He gave me directions. I woke Babe McKenzie and asked if she could take over early.

A bait shop run by a Seminole family marked the place Flagler Bypass forked off U.S. 1. That was where I turned and drove a mile straight into mosquito country. The roofs of fishing camps showed above the brush. There were shanty trailers here, probably a secluded meth lab, maybe a few Conchs proud of having nothing, as if property were a character flaw. The first cars I saw, from the Monroe County Sheriff, blocked both lanes. Past them were cars from the Key West Police, a medical wagon, and a white Ford Bronco with Dade County plates. I parked on the roadside.

Barry Irvington took me into the crime scene. He

was well pressed and sober in an olive poplin suit with a white shirt and a dark tie. His large black loafers were coated with dust.

"Will a dead body upset you?"

Tucked among the slash pine ahead was a rusty SUV with the front doors open. Behind the vehicle, a line of county officers marched out of the deep brush, studying the ground.

"Whose body?" I said. Whoever it was, the sight of a dead person was going to upset me. But I thought I knew the answer. I had Reena Yates on the brain.

"This way."

We walked to the SUV. Bright morning light picked out details of the man sagging in the passenger seat. He had dense blond hair, a lightly creased forehead, straight almost handsome features. He wore a blue-green T-shirt that wasn't clean. One leg of his khaki jeans was black with blood that had leaked down his ankle into a crepe-soled tan shoe. His face bore little expression, as if he no longer minded.

Flies were buzzing in the SUV's interior. The death smell hit me.

"Have you seen him before?" Barry said.

I shook my head. My breakfast, two toaster waffles and orange juice, stirred just below my throat.

"How did he die?" I said.

"He was shot. Come on."

We crossed the ground the search party had covered, and scrub pine gave way to buttonwoods and low brush and then to stumpy mangrove and strangler fig with the bright sky open overhead. A flat metal boat with a small outboard motor was pulled halfway out of a narrow channel onto a gator slide. Flies and beetles crawled over the blood that had thickened in the bottom of the boat.

I refused to go nearer.

"There was shooting out this way the other night. We couldn't pin down the location."

I didn't answer. Several miles of roads separated this nameless key from Bennell's house, but a small boat following the canals that snaked in from the bay might have had to cover half that distance.

Barry pointed down the channel. "They come up here, two of them in the boat. They climb out, but one has been shot and needs support. He's spilling blood all the way to the truck. Pretty far gone, if you figure it's all one guy's blood. While he's sitting in the truck, someone puts a bullet behind his ear and leaves him so an old woman on a nature walk finds him this morning. It was the second morning she had seen the truck."

As he stepped closer to the grounded boat, the flies feeding in the bloody soup seemed to stir with awareness. The thought of them swarming made my skin crawl.

I said: "What's this got to do with me?"

"I thought you might have an idea. No? You're not sure?" He pointed more or less west. "We aren't too far from your client's house."

I didn't ask how he knew who my client was.

"I'm sure I never saw that man before. I'm also sure I didn't shoot him, if that's what's on your mind."

"It's the furthest thing from my mind. But just to prove I'm doing my job, let me see what you're carrying."

I dropped the magazine and cleared the chamber of my small automatic, a .380 Walther that my father had left behind. Barry held the weapon to the light. A gun that hasn't been fired for a while collects a small amount of dust inside the barrel. I hadn't been to the Stock Island range in months and hadn't done any shooting since then. He handed the gun back. He had seen it before, having encouraged me to get a carry permit.

I put the magazine back, slid the gun into the inside-the-pants holster that chafed my side. My father had never been without handguns. The Walther had turned up inside an empty ship's battery after I had looked everywhere else I could think of. It took another day to find its brother, a nine millimeter wrapped in an oily rag and hidden in a false compartment in the cabin roof. Teaching me to shoot had been his idea of father-daughter bonding. I understood some of the symbolism better now than I had at sixteen. I wondered if he had ever understood.

"Who was he?" I asked.

"The vehicle is registered to Brian Voss at a business called Aztec Rarities in Fort Lauderdale. He wasn't carrying any paper, but I think it'll turn out that's who we've got. Stop bullshitting and tell me about the shooting."

"I heard it but I didn't see it."

"Was Commissioner Bennell involved?"

"He had prowlers."

"Let's pretend you tried to reach me to report it. Who did the shooting?"

I told him.

"How many shots?"

"Two from Bennell. Six or eight from the other side."

"What's the rest?"

I told him the rest.

"He said it wasn't Yates on the phone?"

"He said so."

"And you didn't see who was on the boat?"

"I didn't see anyone. Neither did Babe. We were on the other side of the house."

He phoned his department. "Have a car go out to the Yates house in Calusa Estates. See if anyone's home."

They had gotten the dead man out of the SUV onto a stretcher. His arms and knees were frozen in tai-chi motions, an instructor for an audience who didn't care. I had never seen a dead person before. Pushing away Barry's arm, I spun and ran several steps before throwing up. A few people were watching. Nobody laughed.

"I'm impressed you held out so long," Barry said.

A man in a dark suit came over. He had a tight gray face and glossy black hair. "What've you got,

Irv?"

"Possible witness. Megan Trevor, Deputy Chief Pohl. She was working for Commissioner Bennell when he exchanged shots with prowlers."

Pohl's voice became a low rasp. "Why didn't Hub tell us?"

"I'll ask him." Barry told Pohl most of what I'd said while somehow leaving me out of the story.

"I hope Yates hasn't decided to come home," the deputy chief said. "We don't need another round of shit. All right, talk to Hub. Keep *her* away from those two idiots with water pistols."

Barry nodded.

I wondered, What idiots? Then I realized I had already noticed them: two big guys in knit white shirts, who stood on the periphery of the crime scene where they could watch the locals work without getting contaminated. They both wore snug jeans, beepers, badges on their belts, reflective sunglasses. The round-cheeked one looked almost boyish. The older man's face was deeply tanned and heavily pitted around the jaw. Both men wore sporty wristwatches and simple wedding bands. The guys looked like macho jerks, and I wondered what the wives looked like.

"Who are they?" I asked.

"Bureau of Alcohol, Tobacco and Firearms."

"Do they cover shootings?"

"Not much happens that some federal bird doesn't put his nose in."

"Are they the ones with water pistols?"

"If they remembered to bring them."

As we walked to the cars, the baby-faced agent fell into step fifty feet behind us, swimming in a spot of sun glare on a windshield, jumping to a shiny bumper, feet crunching dry grass. When I glanced back, his car keys came out and began bouncing. He was just going about his business. He stopped at the white Bronco with Dade County plates, bent inside and played around in the glove box. I caught that in a side mirror. Then he had a cigarette as he angled onto the road's shoulder, which put him in a good position to check the tag number on Babe's truck.

Blocked by the truck, I got the bag of shell casings from a door pocket and handed it to Barry

Hub Bennell threw me a wounded look when the un-marked police car drove in a minute behind me. He was hosing down the bricks along the seawall. I caught a glimpse of Babe McKenzie running upstairs to collect the top half of her swimsuit.

Barry took an informal statement, collected Hub's .45 as evidence, said nothing about what the com-missioner should or shouldn't have done. I followed Barry back to his car.

"Are you and I okay?" I said.

"Shouldn't we be?" He folded an arm over the car door.

"I could have told you things sooner."

"Next time you will. We're friends. You don't have

to get everything right. I told you that."

Friendship carried a price tag. I wasn't sure what it would be. If he wanted a girlfriend thirty years younger than him, I would have to straighten him out.

"One of the ATF guys took my tag number," I said.

"They collect them because they're professional investigators. They also collect bottle caps, which might contain clues. You ought to stay out of their way."

His phone rang.

9

A skinny policeman climbed out of a patrol car, which was parked halfway up the driveway to the Yates house in Calusa Estates. He spoke with the flat cracker voice I heard only occasionally. The bar above his shirt pocket said Ofc. Brill. "We didn't get an answer at the door or the telephone," he said. "Haven't raised a neighbor who knows anything. Should we go in?"

Peripherally he was watching me, wondering why I was there.

"There's days of mail in the box," he said, trying to tip the decision. "Screen door isn't much."

A man was limping toward us, tall and white-haired, fanning his face with a wide-brimmed straw hat. He wore short sleeves of faded green plaid, white poplin pants that bunched at the waist, tan canvas slip-ons without socks. Everything looked crisp and freshly washed including the old man.

"She's in Gainesville, if you're looking for Mrs. Yates." He spoke directly to Barry. "One of your boys was pounding on my door. I couldn't answer cause I got the trots. I was supposed to collect her mail, but this is the first day I've made it outside. Neoplasms don't leave a man a lot of dignity."

"How long has Mrs. Yates been gone?" Barry asked.

"She left three days after Christmas, visiting parents. She gave me a second-hand fruit cake, as if I could eat such things. All right. She doesn't know."

"Do you have a phone number for her?"

"If you wouldn't mind coming up to my house to get it. I can't walk this far again today. I assume the lady is okay?"

"Some friends hadn't seen her," Barry said. "They were concerned."

"I'm surprised." His long jaw flexed. "I didn't believe she had concerned friends. Once Mr. Yates was gone and the parties stopped, not many people came around. She was even grateful for an ancient neighbor's rare appearances."

"Has her husband been around?"

The old man chuckled. "I haven't seen the jackass. C'mon, I'll get the phone number."

"Go with him," Barry told the policeman. "Where's your partner?"

"Up at the house."

We walked up the driveway. Vegetation grew thick on both sides, creating a semblance of isolation. The house was big and L-shaped, sort of Bahamas Spanish, with tall windows under deep overhangs facing the ocean. An enclosed patio held a dozen gaudy plants in terra cotta urns. A damp breeze rode in on the tide that was smoothing out a small beach a couple hundred feet from the house. A single chaise longue faced the ocean out on the sand.

There was no dead body on the patio curing in the sun. Barry looked through windows, tried doors.

We waited, and eventually Officer Brill came back with a phone number. Barry tried it, and got straight through to Reena Yates. He apologized for disturbing her and hung up.

"Do you want me to drop you in town?" he asked me.

10

Karen Lewis wouldn't let me into the examining room where she performed autopsies. That suited me. We knew each other from Old Town bars, where I enjoyed watching the six-foot raven-haired medical examiner edge out certified stud muffins in the competition for pretty tourists. Karen held an advantage with an endless supply of girl talk, including much about the men who were cruising past. Borrows money. Cries in bed. Tried to rape me in February. Date killers all.

She tossed a photocopy of her report onto the bar. We were at the Turtle Kraals. The late afternoon wind was lifting napkins, fluttering menus.

"Brian Voss, thirty-one years old, Bahia Blanca Apartments, Fort Lauderdale," she said from memory.

"Don't bother to read it. Brian was a bad boy. Puncture wounds inside the elbows. He'd had hepatitis. No HIV, which surprised me. Lesions on left lung, incipient TB. Two kinds of V.D. visible to the unaided eye."

She lifted her draft beer, sipped delicately, and set down the glass. "That's another reason I don't like those little thingos. You never know where one's been—in this, up that. No thanks, guys. This man had a good strong body and abused the hell out of it."

"Did you recover a bullet?"

"Just one, probably twenty-two caliber long judging by the weight. It banged around inside the cranium for a while. More or less instantly fatal."

"More or less?"

"You'd have to ask him if he felt anything or had a thought. He might have noticed a lot of circuits going black at the same time."

"There wasn't a bullet in his leg?"

"No. There was a big nasty entry wound, a clipped artery, then a mother of an exit hole. The projectile was already wobbling when it hit him."

"So you don't know the caliber."

She gave me a professional squint. "I could testify as an expert that the wound is consistent with a heavy, slow-moving slug, most likely a forty-five. The cops say he was in a boat?"

"They found him in his truck. But there was a boat nearby with blood on the bottom."

"He would have bled as long as he had a pulse."

She dived a fried shrimp into hot sauce. "So what are you doing these days?"

"Same old."

"Someone told me you shacked up with an artist."

"He's moved on."

"So is there hope for someone who cares about you?"

"You don't care about me, Karen, you're a hound. Also, you're not a guy."

She made a face. "I autopsy more men than women. There's nothing special about them."

"They're special at being assholes."

She nodded firmly. "There you go. They've got that down pat. But it works to my advantage. You'd be surprised how often. I've got a very sympathetic ear."

I glanced at the written report on the autopsy, handed it back to Karen.

"Next time I'm broken-hearted, I'll call you," I said.

"You're a tease."

I called Bennell and gave him the news .

"You sure my shot didn't kill him?" He sounded relieved for the first two words, then halfway disappointed.

"He would have bled to death from it, but somebody preempted that outcome."

"I never took a shot at anyone before this," he mumbled. "I hired a lawyer, Woody Erskine, just in case things get bad. He cussed me for talking to the police before bringing him in."

"It would have looked worse if you had refused to talk."

"That's what I told him, being a commissioner and all. Erskine asked if my political image was worth heavy jail time. He has a point."

I was still at the Turtle Kraals, nursing another soft drink as the afternoon crowd got comfortable. In a couple of hours we could start thinking of ourselves as the late-afternoon crowd, which was only a short step from becoming the evening crowd. The comatose crowd. I didn't want to be there then.

"The man you shot was named Brian Voss. Does that ring a bell?"

It took him a while to say, "Yeah."

"Tell me."

"He's got an import business, him and a partner. I remember them from a party the Yateses threw. The mayor was showing off some antique piece he'd bought."

"Recently?"

"Year and a half, I guess. Only reason I remember is Voss was one of the names the federal people hit me with. Was supposed to shake me out of my trousers. They wanted to know how long had we been doing business, Voss and me. That sort of stuff. Suppose I'll be hearing it all again thanks to you."

"Why would Voss come after you with a gun?"

"It doesn't make sense, kid. I got nothing of his.

There's no reason for him to think otherwise."

"Who was his business partner?"

"Latin fellow named Avila. He handled the import side."

11

The Overseas Highway runs exactly one hundred nine miles over a total of forty-one bridges from the tip of Key West to the causeway that bends north exiting the Keys for Florida City and Miami. For much of the distance the road is two lanes wide. A collision at any of those bottlenecks stalls traffic for hours. Brush fires up in the Everglades can close the road for days. In Hub Bennell's convertible, I made good time all the way to Fort Lauderdale. A seedy commercial strip along the airport highway, where the anchor tenant was a closed-up strip joint, had a glass door brightly lettered AZTEC RARITIES INC. above a little painted sombrero The shop's windows were hung with craft paper, and the door was locked with the solid feel of not having been opened in a while.

So Voss's business sucked. So had the strip club's. So did mine.

It was getting dark, which made the Bahia Blanca Marina Towers easy to find, the lights of two twenty-story buildings like a fireworks display against the Atlantic sky. As soon as I drove up, I had trouble picturing a drug addict living there unless he had a lot of money. A woman in the marina's office, all brown and bouncy under silver hair, said she had never heard of Bahia Blanca Apartments. "This is the Towers, dear."

As the door opened behind me, she spoke louder. "We provide an elegant and charmingly upscale lifestyle available to only the very best people."

A yachtsman coming in, wearing a cravat decorated with signal flags and a matching pocket square in a white blazer, seemed unimpressed to hear this. His chin thrust ahead, cutting off the smaller vessels, his gait determined, he had the slightly frantic look of someone trapped on a five-million-dollar yacht with a broken icemaker.

"No mail today, Mr. Conarky," she said.

He pivoted without a word and headed back out, and the woman leaned toward me and whispered, "There might be an apartment building by that name out toward the airport, but definitely not around *here*."

"Thanks," I said.

Heading out, I admired the money snuggled up against the brightly lighted piers. If I sailed my father's boat in here, the neighbors would sink of embarrassment.

The Bahia Blanca Apartments were a dozen blocks from where I had started. A line of small shops occupied the first floor of a long building on Southeast Sixth, and the second floor had apartments that could be reached from outside staircases at either end of the building. The apartments would have a water view if a hurricane brought the Atlantic Ocean a mile inland.

Diagonally across the street, a white Ford Bronco was three-quarters hidden in an alley. I drove up to Eighth, came around and parked a block north. From there I could see the Bronc's white rear-end sticking out. It could have been anyone's ride. Maybe it was the ATF boys, maybe not. As long as it faced into the alley, the occupants couldn't see me unless someone was crouched back in the stowage area.

I sat and watched the Bahia Blanca Apartments. I had no plan beyond getting a look at Voss's surroundings and maybe his partner. Where either Voss or his partner fit into Hub's problems I hadn't a clue. If they'd sold antiques to Mayor Yates, it was possible they thought he had money stashed. Or knew he did. And imagined Hub had a piece of it . . . or knew he did.

Not many people were out walking. A man was waiting in a motel driveway, away from the office, dark hair, dark slacks, dark T-shirt, a longneck and a cigarette in the same hand, touching one and then the other to his lips. He didn't seem to be paying attention to anything. The BMW's top was down, which made me feel a little exposed. Salsa music had been bumping the air for a while when a car passed on the avenue. The neighborhood was just a little too seedy. The building fronting the sidewalk was a little too dark. A girl in a convertible was going to attract attention. It happened almost immediately.

A lowrider squealed to a stop and a man with black whiskers framing bee-stung lips grinned at me from low in the passenger seat.

"Hey, *puta*, you eat sausage?"

He laughed at the driver, looked back at me.

"You don' eat *concha*, do you?"

If he showed any sign of getting out of the car, I was going to lift the Walther two inches so he could see it pointing at his mouth. But if I did that, he might get out of the car anyway just to prove he was *muy macho* or whatever he needed to prove, and then we would have a problem.

"Je ne parle pas Anglais," I said.

They laughed and drove off.

I gave it a minute to prove I wasn't worried but not long enough for them to come back. I could hear the shrill, rapid horns, the screaming pretty voice, and the pattering drums as they cruised the neighborhood. They would be back, couldn't resist. A U-turn got me away from the curb. I went north on Federal Highway for a few blocks, turned onto Las Olas and headed east, the music still with me, making me a little happy as I drifted along the marinas and beaches on North Atlantic until the right sort of place beckoned. When I drove the BMW under the valet awning, I handed over the keys just as if I'd done it a hundred times. My table was on a deck cantilevered over the sand facing the ocean. Just the place for a rum-something after selling a two-million-dollar condo, which along this stretch would be a fixer-upper. A volleyball game down on the beach competed with the surf sound. I treated myself to stone crab and mango salad, accepting the prices in stoic silence. Other people had money, I could pretend to. After dinner I sat around nursing a diet ginger ale. Nobody tried to pick me up. Nobody asked me to dance to the mambo music, which was only in my head.

At one-fifteen I drove through Voss's neighborhood again. The white Bronco was gone. So was the music. I parked where I had before, with the top up. The nearest street lamp was half a block away; none of the light reached inside the car. Daddy Trevor would have been reasonably proud.

The next part took forty minutes, about five minutes longer than I had patience. Then the man on the second floor balcony of the Bahia Blanca Apartments, who must have stood in the shadows a while, moved to a door I assumed was Voss's. A car passed on the street when he was looking out from the balcony, and faint reflected light caught his face. I couldn't tell much except that the face was narrow. Even that could have been a trick of the light. But it made me think of the man who had hung out in the motel's driveway. If this was the same man, he had outwaited the ATF pair.

So he was patient, big deal.

He entered the apartment, shut the door, and a wash of light appeared at the top of a window. I sat and thought about things. Like where he'd been before I saw him on the balcony. Like who was the more experienced hunter. Definitely not I. After a while I got jumpy. I could watch the apartment door, and I could check the car's rear and side mirrors for someone creeping up behind me, but I couldn't cover both at the same time. There were scraggly palms lining the avenue. Once I started paying attention to them, it was easy to imagine a shadow behind this one or that one. It was like this on the boat some nights. A bump or a creak I couldn't account for and suddenly I was wide awake staring at the hatch, checking every porthole for a face, wondering if some of my father's old enemies hadn't heard he was gone. Two weeks ago I'd had a gun in my hand by the time I understood it was Tim stumbling around in the dark in the cockpit. A good thing I hadn't been able to see our future that night.

A security gig at a Key West supermarket was one thing. Nobody in his right mind pulled a stickup in the Lower Keys, where there was only one road out, so my big-time criminals were shoplifters and men's room Romeos. This was different. Whoever had snuck up onto the balcony was used to moving unobserved. He was arguably good at something a shoplifter wasn't.

I looked up at the balcony. While I had squirmed, the light in the apartment had gone out. I didn't know if he'd slipped out the door, but I'd had enough for one night.

I spent a toss-and-turn night in a motel far enough up the coast that I should have been thinking about new things. But I thought about a man creeping along in the dark. I thought about the emptiness of my boat. And then I stopped my wakeful thinking and dreamt about my father, who was a skinny gunslinger, and I got a chance to tell him he should have stayed with us longer, should have loved Mom and me better, .but I was crying so hard the whole thing only confused him. We were sailing as I tried to explain all this, the water dark under us, and then I was still on the boat but sailing alone.

12

It *didn't seem* so bad in the morning. The Atlantic was flashing on distant highrises, and palmetto shadows striped the roads. There were no dark corners around the shabby apartment building, nobody staking the place out except me. The woman in the next unit was on her way to work when I knocked on Voss's door at quarter after eight. She had big arms, a haystack of yellow hair, and when I showed her my license and said I was trying to collect a few hundred dollars on behalf of a company that had sold office supplies to her neighbor, she was happy to tell me I was out of luck.

"You're too late," she said. "Brian got himself killed down in the Keys."

"That's terrible."

"Yes, I'm sure it is." She gave me a second look, decided I was a benign form of life for a bill collector. "Brian's partner might want to settle your account. I'm not saying he will, but he's a nice young man, Mr. Hoya. A very sweet man. I told him he should never have gotten involved with Brian."

"Why is that?"

"Well, you have it right there—he owes money. People like Brian use up the kind people around them." Her face softened. "If he hadn't lost his life, Brian would have ended his days in a rescue mission. And there aren't many of them around here, so he might have been the street."

"I guess getting killed saved him from that."

"If it comes to it, I'll take the street," she said. "And if I stand here blabbing much longer, Mr. Aaron might take his wonderful job back, then I'll lose all this."

"Where can I find Mr. Hoya?"

"Probably at their place of business. It's a few blocks from here." She gave me the address of Aztec Rarities. "I don't think they're doing too well, but if it's just Mr. Hoya now, that might change."

I followed her downstairs. After she drove off in an old Plymouth, I went back up and slipped the latch on Voss's apartment. He had kept his bad habits in plain sight. A brandy bottle in the front room, a hypodermic syringe on the bedroom bureau, packs of rubbers like red bunting over a bed post, Star Wars paperbacks on a nightstand, a DVD titled *Boots'n Spurs* atop a tiny TV. The bed smelled foul from five feet away, which was as close as I got.

Light came into the kitchen through a curtainless back window. Dishes in the sink were covered in black mold. A souvenir bar rag from a Lauderdale beach saloon hung above the sink on thumb tacks. I imagined the man I had seen dead pushing tacks into the wall to decorate his rooms. A lidded tin that had held a bottle of expensive whiskey stood on the counter, the painted guardsman lifting his pike. I pictured Voss opening the tin, removing the bottle with a flourish, toasting the holiday. Not used to looking at dead people's things, I wanted to personalize everything as I had with my father's junk. Every dirty sock told a story if you let it. Someone visiting this apartment before me had raised the lid on the tin and observed the white powder caked in the corners. That was what I should be doing, observing what was there—not reacting emotionally to it.

I went back to the front room and peeked out at the balcony. It was empty.

The apartment had been thoroughly searched, furniture disarranged, dresser drawers tipped out, sofa cushions sliced open on the floor, blue jeans and a few shirts dumped from the single closet. The bathroom mirror had been shattered, the larger pieces stacked in the wash basin. It was one way to check what was behind the glass. The lid was off the toilet tank. Short of pulling up the linoleum or knocking out the walls, I didn't know what more they could have done.

If the police or ATF agents had done the search, it seemed like a lot of effort spent on a loser.

Standing in the middle of the front room, with its dusty blinds and ruined furniture, I did a three-sixty turn. I didn't know what I was supposed to notice. The apartment stank, but anyone with a cat box has smelled worse. But maybe this particular stink should tell me something. Lem Rees at the Carbuncle claimed he could smell when a woman had had sex in the preceding twenty-four hours. Though I didn't believe him, I had stayed away from the Carbuncle after Tim and I spent a playful morning.

I went back into the bedroom, put the back of my hand against the bedsheet. It wasn't warm, but it felt damp. The magazine on the floor was open to a two-page display of three men, representing considerable ethnic diversity, engaged in what I guessed you would call copulation. All they needed to liven it up were a dog, a pony and a postman. The images were wrinkled in spots where the paper had gotten wet.

In the bathroom, I noticed what I should have noticed the first time, water beads in the shower and a damp towel on the rack.

Last night's visitor had stayed a while.

From the bathroom doorway I could see most of the bedroom and half the front room. Unlimbering my gun, I tried to decide if I was alone. The water beads were drying, and the stringy towel could have been used hours ago. There was no room in the closet for an occupant. No place in the front room or the kitchen—except a contortionist might be hiding in the cabinet under the sink. Still in the doorway, I squatted so I could see under the bed.

Then I stood up and headed for the front door. It was like being five years old again and tiptoeing past dark rooms. The gun still had the safety on, with my thumb against it. Dad and the Stock Island range master both would be proud. There are a lot of niceties to consider before shooting someone in an apartment you've burglarized.

I was heading home through glamorous, overbuilt, thoroughly congested Islamorada, where the brave tarpon is no match for the sunburned visitor with hair on his shoulders. A wobbling boat full of such visitors passed under the bridge at Teatable Key Channel, heading for blue water, deep sea rods raised like spears, a boombox thumping the rhythm of their war drums. The phone went off, and I heard Gloria Hutchin asking if I felt like lunch. "I've been talking to the old Hubster," she said, "and I think I may be able to help."

13

She was sitting in the full sun on the south-facing deck at Bogie's Fish House. At half-past eleven, the parking lot at the twenty-mile marker was nearly full, and all the outdoor tables were taken. A waiter was trading Gloria's tall empty glass for a slippery new one. A breeze was tugging her bright green scarf and whipping her hair. She looked at me over amber sunglasses. Her lips were a glossy red so deep it was almost brown. "The first thing you have to understand," she said as I was sitting down, "is that Cole Yates is an absolute shit in every way imaginable."

"I have a big imagination," I said.

She waved her fingers. "Here young man, bring the lady a—what, a Margarita?"

"Diet ginger ale," I said before he ran off.

"Pooh! You're not enjoying life, Megan. Where's the *joie de vivre*? The devil may care? At your age, I was dancing all night. There was a whole year when I don't think I was ever sober—a fine year; we split the summer between the Cape and Block Island and drank away the winter in Miami and Havana." Her face pulled down on one side, smiling. "When things became difficult later, I was grateful for those memories. No matter that most of them were out of focus."

"It sounds like you had a bigger spending allowance than I got."

"Nonsense, I let my men pay. You're cuter than I was, with your little ponytail and pretty eyes. If they've got to have it, let them pay for it." She sipped her drink. "You've just let yourself go too cheap."

At the next table, three middle-aged couples in sailcloth shirts and shorts talked loudly about the next leg down the Intracoastal. All their faces wore the roughened blush of serious boaters. Several big-shouldered cruisers were tied at Bogie's pier. Another round of drinks arrived, and the boaters sat back with a collective sigh.

Gloria shook her head, still on Topic Megan. "That painter, my God! I wouldn't have let him paint my toenails. Was he something special in the sack?"

I didn't answer.

"Well?"

"No." There are guys, like Tim, who could make a corpse come but aren't special.

"You were studying literature in school, weren't

you? So I guess you're soft on the artsy-fartsy types. It's too bad they're so poor."

"It's too bad I'm so poor," I said, "which is why I'm working for Mr. Bennell."

"Poor Hubbard is so afraid for his reputation. When he called me yesterday, wanting advice, I had to pry the facts out of him. He didn't admit hiring you until this morning. As if I could help him without knowing any of the circumstances."

"I've had the same problem."

"I have one advantage you lack. I know Cole Yates very, very well. Don't get wide-eyed, I don't mean that. Our political objectives clashed a few times. I was in a group that circulated petitions asking the city to preserve the last few undeveloped parcels of land on the island. As mayor, Cole challenged a few hundred of our signatures and poof went the petition drive. He was a prick when it came to getting his way." I noticed she had slipped into the past tense. Sipping her drink, she looked at me over the sunglasses again. "Cole believes a piece of land is unhappy if it doesn't have a building on it. He used to ask developers for five percent to make sure the permitting process encountered no sudden obstacles."

"He took bribes?"

"Consulting fees. Nobody thinks it's a good idea to criminalize useful commercial arrangements. Then some uncouth ass from outside perhaps asks how cozy is too cozy."

"Is that what the feds were doing?"

"I think so."

"Is Mr. Bennell involved?"

"What did he tell you?"

"Born innocent, still innocent."

She laughed. "Well, maybe he is."

"Do you think he has Mayor Yates's money?"

Her lopsided smile came again. "Hubbard is an old friend. None of my old friends are choir boys. If Cole shared a little good luck with a city commissioner, it wouldn't surprise me. Keeping it all for himself would be bad manners. Nobody likes a pig."

"Mr. Bennell said it never happened."

"Did he? Dear Hubbard is crafty but he isn't terribly well organized. When he tells fibs, he's never thinking more than one step ahead. That's fine with me, because it's easy to keep up with him."

She consulted the menu that lay beside her glass.

"Do you like grouper, Megan? Most locals don't, because the grouper feeds at the bottom. It seems a silly distinction to me." She flicked a glance at the waiter, who veered toward us. "This is my treat, so don't hold back."

I ordered grouper without looking at the menu.

"I've still got a few official contacts," she said. "Aunt Gloria can find out if there's still federal interest in either Cole or Hub. Strictly for your benefit, Megan, in case you need to get out of the way."

"Thank you."

"My pleasure. You know, I don't believe I'm para-noid—though I've a right to be. But the way it added up, I always felt Cole was dead. He left town too fast. Didn't come back to collect his winnings. The man could fast-talk you out of your pants and you would never notice a draft. Does that sound like a person who would leave his money behind?"

"I've heard there may not have been much money after debts were paid."

"That's one of the semi-official versions, Megan. Personally, I don't trust it."

14

My client wasn't home and he wasn't at the charter office. He wasn't answering any of the phone numbers I tried.

"If I see him," said Luis, the Cuban pilot, "what shall I tell him?"

"Ask him to call me."

He answered with a thumbs-up. "Okay. Captain Steve will be sorry he missed you." He meant the other pilot, the young, bold one.

I said, "'Captain' Steve?"

"I assign him the rank. Sounds good, huh? Captain Steve Taylor. Most ladies are impressed."

"Most of them."

He shrugged. "Those who have romance in their souls."

"Does that let me out?"

"I think so," Luis said.

I drove to Hawkes Marina, parked close to the dock and hoped neither Arthur Hawkes nor his mother took the BMW as evidence I had come into money. They had always been relaxed when I was a few days late paying the slip fees. I went aboard the boat.

There was always a ghost present. He had never apologized for his long absences. A child who was worth anything could raise hell herself, that was his excuse. He had been an orphan and it hadn't hurt him. He was too old for children anyway, forty-seven when I was born, too late for him to enjoy the companionship of someone whose only claim on him was blood. God knew what he thought my mother's claim had been. Even weaker.

I had to add up the years to appreciate the implausible truth, that this indestructible man had been sixty-nine at his death. The summer before, when I spent two months on the boat, he had looked little different from the man who had been so irresistible to my mother a long time ago.

Daddy Longlegs I had called him when I was small. He had towered.

A lot of myths about Danny Trevor floated around the Lower Keys. Most of them were hard to credit, and I didn't like asking people who had known him. *I* should have been able to sort out what was true. Had he really flown Fidel Castro's sister on the first leg of her trip into exile? Had he directed the dirty work in

Grenada days before the Marines landed? He had never told me. The stories other people told failed to add up to a truth I wanted. When you got past the covert operations, the booze, the slovenly habits, you had a dreadful husband and a haphazard father. Last night, in the motel fifteen miles outside Fort Lauderdale, with a beer party thumping beyond the thinly partitioned wall, I had spent too long thinking about him and ended up wasting tears. Tears were always wasted, according to Dad.

Then—eyes closed, I was out on the Gulf alone, in the slippery light, sensing large things swimming under the surface, changing shape as they rose out of the shadows to get me.

Coming out of the dream, I told myself to be practical. They had gotten *him*. There was nothing to be done about it.

For a while I threw things around the boat's cabin in a pretense of straightening up. Thinking about Hub Bennell didn't improve my mood. The way he had been ready for the intruders in the motorboat, having covered himself with hired security because of how worried he was, but waiting for them, pretending he was a fat sad boob—all that made it easy to picture him shucking Cole Yates out of his money. And not impossible to picture him dumping Yates into a canal. But if that had happened, would he have mentioned either money or Yates to me?

Gloria's answer could be tweaked to cover that. Hub was crafty but short-sighted. She was also right about something else. If Hub and Yates had gone wading together in the deep water, I wanted no part of the consequences.

I dug the ringing phone out of my pocket, expecting my client.

"Reena Yates is back safe and sound from Gainesville," Barry Irvington said. "Knowing your concern, I thought you should know. Have you had lunch?"

"Yes."

"Are you still drinking ginger ale?"

"Mostly."

"I can afford that. Meet me at Pepe's. You don't need a lift?"

I said I didn't. I puttered some more on the boat. When the cabin looked almost respectable—all the dirty clothes piled in one place—I felt a sudden urge to call Mom and tell her how neat things were. I went up on deck with the phone, sat on the cabin roof and took account of life at the marina. Bright clean afternoon, sky deep and reaching, nobody on the walkways, little action on neighboring decks. The seabirds perching on deck rails were so still they could have been carvings. I felt reluctant to disturb this temporarily becalmed state, so I didn't call.

At Pepe's we sat at the outdoor bar. The last time Tim and I had been here, we had rated people coming through the door. Good company meant she had never thrown up on a pizza. Bad company cried over former lovers.

"Are you sure Mrs. Yates was up north?" I asked

Barry.

"She has relatives in Gainesville. The old man's story checked." He leaned close to the zinc counter, trying to create a space of intimacy between us.

"I mean, could she have been with her husband?"

"Sure she could. We don't have her under surveillance. Look, you may have a problem. The department got an inquiry about you."

"What inquiry?"

"You were observed attempting to contact a criminal suspect in Lauderdale. The people watching him want to know—and I quote—if 'she's as dirty as her old man.'" He lifted his bottle, took a small drink. "I told them you were a model citizen. That probably put you on the ATF shit list, given their view that I'm in somebody's pocket."

"I was staking Voss's place. I didn't think they'd noticed me."

"Why were you doing it?"

"Voss and his partner knew the mayor."

"Who is the partner?"

"A neighbor said his name was Hoya. Hub told me something different, a Latino named Avila. Their store, Aztec Rarities, was closed. It looked like they were out of business."

"How does Bennell know them?"

"He said he saw Voss and Avila at a party at Yates's house. The mayor was showing off antiques."

"Yates and his wife collected pre-Columbian art. I'll see if the name Hoya turns up anything."

"Or Avila."

"Him, too."

"I saw someone go into Voss's apartment after the ATF left." I described the man who had slipped through the shadows.

"Could you identify him?"

"No."

"Voss's companion the other night is probably the person who killed him," Barry said. He gave me the hard stare of a high school guidance counselor urging abstinence. "You may want to think about that."

I thought about it.

"If it was Hoya or Avila," Barry said, "he put a bullet in the head of his partner and left him to be found."

"Not subtle."

"Keep something else in mind. The ATF agents who asked after you have a grudge against your father. Randy Nash does especially."

"Which one is he?"

"Younger one."

"Tell me."

"Last summer   Nash searched your dad's boat without a warrant. Danny came home and caught him. So a few night owls got to see an ATF agent marched up the pier with his pants around his ankles."

Instead of saying anything, I sipped ginger ale in which the ice was melting. When he got impatient with the silence, Barry said: "If Nash had anything on Danny, he'd have charged him. He didn't."

"What did he think he had?"

"Nash doesn't confide in me."

He pushed his bottle in a small circle. His gaze followed its motion in a way that took in most of our surroundings. The bartender was near the kitchen door. An old man in a Habana Libre shirt was four seats away reading the *Citizen*. A couple who were sitting nearby on a bench awaiting a dinner table were talking about reef diving.

"Stay away from him. He cuts corners. Even his partner knows it."

I knew it took a lot for one cop to badmouth another, even a fed, to a civilian.

"Why is ATF interested in Voss?" I persisted.

"They don't tell me that, either. Whatever it is, you need to stay out of their way."

I stopped at the air charter office on the way home. Luis was still in charge. Captain Steve was entertaining pretty tourists in the Dry Tortugas. Hub had not returned. I had phoned Babe's apartment and gotten a meow'rl answer. Bennell's cell phone number had given me a businesslike notice that the customer wasn't available.

With a helpful grin, Luis added, "The two *federales* who were here when you last visited are gone away."

"What are you talking about?"

"They were there"—pointing to a stand of slash pine—"in their big white SUV watching everyone. They came in after you left and asked for my papers."

Lowering his lids over bright eyes, he said, "I tell them I am a naturalized citizen of the United States. I don't even say *Estados Unidos*. The young one says half the *putas* in Miami claim that. *Maricon*. So I show him my papers."

"What did they want?"

"Where could they find Mr. Bennell? I tell them try his house. For some reason, I forget to mention his other business."

"I need to find him, too," I said.

"He may be at his boats. He has a fishing charter business on Key Vaca. He makes money at that, perhaps. This business sucks bigtime." He leaned forward on the counter. "Maybe I buy these sissy planes and we go bomb Havana. What do you say?"

"Do you have a phone number for the boats?"

He scribbled a number on a small square of blue paper that said BENNELL'S AIR CHARTER at the top. When I tried the number he'd written, it rang a dozen times before I gave up.

"Where on Key Vaca?" I said.

On the way, I remembered the name of the lawyer my client had hired. Woody Erskine, a go-to guy in town who liked to take care of things away from the courtroom. Hub might ditch me and his pilots and still keep in touch with the lawyer. I phoned as I drove, got an answering machine and asked Erskine to call me if he heard from Hub.

15

Right off the Seven-mile Bridge, I began looking for a turn. It was late afternoon, and wind batted against my sunglasses. Half the sport fishermen from the northern forty-eight had converged on these ugly few miles of motels, charter boat companies, carry-out fish windows and bait-and-beer shacks that made up charmless, asphalt-flat Key Vaca. The place had even lost its name to the unincorporated city sprawling across the island and most people now called it Marathon. A man and a woman wearing pink windbreakers walked onto the highway in front of me as if vacationers were a protected species like the Key Deer. I hit the brake, found my side street, and followed it to a large busy marina.

The signs out front said Sailhook. Both the aqua

boards and the glittery word "Sailhook" bent in the middle like leaping fish. Cars and vans nudged a long rope railing that stretched a couple of city blocks. Pennants flapped. Clouds sent fast-moving shadows across the pavement. A half-dozen teenagers marched ahead of me like pall-bearers sharing the weight of three large insulated coolers. Coming down the main ramp from the marina, a small bald man stepped out of the procession's way, making a show of paying his respects, keeping an arm around the waist of the young woman beside him who wore a man's white shirt, a bikini bottom and heeled clogs.

The marina was laid out like a village square, with a grocery and a chandler's sharing one building, a chain restaurant and a seafood bar at two opposing corners, and a small brick building strung with maritime flags near the entrance. The small brick building was the office. On three sides, piers and lesser walkways stretched off providing slips for more boats than I could count. Hawkes Marina would have been lost in a corner of this operation. Electronic gear on the bigger ships bristled against the sky.

The office was empty, with two phones ringing. I intercepted a man in a blue Sailhook shirt outside who said he hadn't seen Bennell today. I swept a hand around. "Is Mr. Bennell the owner?"

"Of Sailhook? Not hardly. Mr. Bennell has a couple boats we handle for him." He called to a woman approaching the docks, "Hey, Becks! Is Hub Bennell around?"

As she shook her head and kept moving, he made a dash for the office. I hurried to catch up with Becks. She said, "One of his boats, *Flyboy*, just came in over in B Section. You might find him there."

Flyboy was a small sportfisher with a deck full of unstowed gear and one middling big dead tarpon. A man wearing a fierce sunburn stood shirtless, legs splayed, protecting the kill.

There was no sign of my client. The next slip was occupied by a flat-bottomed *Keys Pilot*, which also sounded like Bennell's. The tarpaulin-shaded deck was empty. The next two slips were unoccupied. Then came a fat cruiser and a houseboat, neither bearing a name that suggested flight. I went back to the *Flyboy*. Climbing down from an elevated bridge, a man with a blond beard shouted orders to the two crew. He wore white shorts and a crisp white shirt with shoulder boards that could have gotten him mistaken for a regular Navy man.

I waved. "Is Mr. Bennell on board?"

He gave a curt head shake before coming over to the railing. His face was deeply lined. "He should have been here this morning. The gal who showed up for the job couldn't wait forever." He wagged a thumb at the other boat. "The *Pilot* needs a skipper and mate for snorkel trips. We thought we had a skipper but the boss forgot to show. Are you looking for the same job?"

I lifted my sunglasses. "I'm not sure."

"If you're hard up for work, it's okay. But there've

got to be better hitches. He didn't bring the pay last night, so my men are bitching. I tell them we get paid or we strip his boat."

I put my sunglasses back down. If Bennell was missing appointments, I knew the most likely distraction, which meant I couldn't afford to work with Babe again. She wagged her tail, and I chased mine. Only Luis's offhand remark had brought me here. If I didn't find Hub this afternoon, he would find me when he wanted his car back. Then I could give him my report and a bill. I headed for the marina gate.

I went down the ramp to the parking area. There was a long stretch on the eastern side where a small canal ran beside the parking rope. I was closing in on the BMW when I looked up. There was a man in the marina just drawing back from a railing. I caught a flash of glossy black hair, long lips, olive skin—silky black shirt, linen trousers, not typical marina wear even among the rich and Latin. I couldn't tell where he was looking because rectangular amber Revos hid his eyes. I thought there was a good chance he had been watching me.

I spun and ran back to the ramp. By the time I reached the top, he was out of sight. Walking along the concrete piers, I phoned Barry.

"I'm at Sailhook marina in Marathon," I said. "The man I saw last night is here."

"I thought you couldn't identify him."

"Now I can, I've seen him closer."

If he'd killed Voss, I'd probably gotten as close as I

wanted to.

"Where is he, right now?" Barry said.

"I've lost sight of him."

"If you find him, don't confront him. What do you think he's doing there?"

"I don't know."

"He probably followed you."

I didn't say anything. But thought: *Followed me from where, and how long?*

Shit.

If he'd picked me up outside Voss's apartment this morning, I had led him everywhere I hoped to find my client. Right down into Key West, to Bennell's house, to the air charter office.

And, of course, to my boat. But Voss and his killer hadn't come looking for me the other night. They'd come after my client. I owed Hub and Babe a heads-up.

16

Easier said than done. For fifteen minutes of useless phoning, I kept only half an eye on the road behind me. Then I gave up. It was nearly dusk when I crossed the last bridge into Key West and drove down Truman Avenue and parked on Whitehead Street in front of Babe McKenzie's building.

She had three rooms on the top floor in a mansion with loose shutters and buckled gutters, where mammoth Poincianas bowed on either side of the front steps. She called down the inside stairs and when I reached the apartment's doorway she stood barefoot, with a small calico cat tying imaginary knots around her ankles. Her hair was wrapped in a towel, her breasts swung like boxing gloves in a sweater, and she lifted a tall glass full of ice and bourbon.

"Sure you won't?" she said.

"Not today," I said. "Have you got any idea where my client is?"

"Why don't you sit down, have a drink and wait an hour. Not being falsely modest, I 'spect he'll be here."

I had reached her by phone while I was still twenty minutes up the highway but hadn't filled her in.

"Hub didn't show for an appointment in Marathon this morning, and I think one of the men from the other night has been following me."

Before I could remind her she was supposed to be babysitting the client, Babe said, "He said he had business." She was blinking to focus. The tall bourbon count wasn't at one, or two, this afternoon. "Told me to go home and he'd take care of it. Don't think he wants protection anymore."

He probably felt he could shoot it out with anyone who came around, having scored a hit the first time.

"What business?"

"Had to meet some fellow. Then hire someone for a boat. Did you know he's got boats?"

"How's he getting around?"

"He borrowed my truck. I've got a job tomorrow where I'll need my wheels, unless I tell them to stuff it. I'm trying to make up my mind."

"You haven't married him yet, you know."

"Just daydreaming. Hubby Bear has some fine qualities."

"He likes your chest."

"He does that."

"So where is he?"

She frowned. "Tonight? He wanted to talk to this Curtis fellow down at the city marina. Poor sweetie's still obsessed about the mayor."

"What's one got to do with the other?"

"Honey, cussing the mayor ain't my idea of pillow talk, so I just tuned that part out. Why are you so eager?"

"I think Hub needs to hear about a guy who may have been with Voss."

"Let's go see Curtis," Babe said. Shuffling across the pine floor, she deposited her drink on a table, bent over a cat pan and shook out her hair. She pulled on pink tennis shoes, stuffed money and her gun into a little straw purse. "Tell me I don't look like a hooker."

"Not without high heels."

"I'll just leave a note for Hubby Bear. You got me a little worried, sugar. Anything happens to that big boob, I'm going to be a fry cook when I'm fifty. Tell me you know that's a long way off."

"It's a long way off," I said.

In cut-off jeans, a Hog's Breath Saloon shirt and sandals, Curtis Humphrey, the city's assistant harbor master, stood about five feet four inches tall with vestiges of hair clinging to the top of a perfectly round head, whiskers prickling his throat, and patches of broken veins flushing his cheeks. He seemed to be sweating gin. I got upwind and pretended interest as he pointed with the pride of near-possession to some of the hundred footers berthed at the city marina.

"Prince Bandar owns her, that little Feadship. Captain says she's as fast as a Persian whore."

"Is that fast?" inquired Babe.

"That's Rockabilly Bob's boat. And Dirty Gertie says she saw Cher on that thing over there with all the frou-frou. Personally I doubt it."

I said, "Did Commissioner Bennell come see you today?"

"I don't believe, ladies, the effing fool has ever come to see me."

"Crap," said Babe.

"As may be," he agreed. His glance wandered between us, chest to chest. My T-shirt could have used a bra, but he settled fondly on Babe's sweater, which wobbled every time she spoke.

"Didn't you come to City Hall wanting to talk to Mr. Bennell?" Babe insisted.

"Ma'am, one of us is in a time warp." He angled a bare eyebrow at her. "From that hairdo you've got, I'm pretty sure it's you."

"Curtis," I said, "did Commissioner Bennell come to see you?"

"I already told you, no. Now, approximately six months ago, as the blond goddess implies, having it all slightly backward, I had occasion to point out to Mr. Bennell a small oddity at the marina. He ignored me, just as if I were a no-account drunk. Can you imagine?"

"Just barely," Babe said.

"What oddity?"

"More a coincidence, perhaps." Waiting to be prompted, he ran a finger under his nose and squinted back at me with a sudden look of recognition.

Before he could say anything, I prodded him, "What was the coincidence?"

"Same two queens stopped here three times, about a month apart, bringing different boats through. That's three times that I noticed. Two of the boats were in the millionaires club. The last one wasn't much. I thought it was suspicious. Commissioner Bennell thought they were in the repositioning business."

"What did you think they were doing?"

"Bringing in smokeable imports was my guess." A shrug stretched him an inch taller. "I get paid to collect dock fees and see the rules abided by. The marina ordinances don't specifically say you can't run dope through here."

"Can you describe the men?"

"Boat niggers." The term referred to people who took crew jobs to get from one place to another, or to have a place to sleep. "Course, they could have been university graduates like me. One fella was blond, one Chicano-type."

"Have you seen them again?"

"Nope. So maybe I was wrong. Or they heard someone was raising questions and moved on. Or they got busted." Considering the possibilities, he drew a flat bottle from the back pocket of his shorts and took a sip.

Babe looked at me and shrugged. We couldn't see what it had to do with Hub.

"So why are you and Blondie asking after the commissioner?" he said.

Babe answered. "None of your business, you old stinkpot."

Curtis Humphrey shook his head. "You should work on that hostility, Blondie. Your young friend here—she ever tell you she shucked off her clothes for the gentlemen at Blackbeards? As I remember," he said, winking at me, "this pretty little thing's got freckles on her tits."

Babe looked at me. I shrugged. Not every drunk had been too drunk to remember.

17

"*I didn't know* about that," Babe said. "Blackbeards is a hole."

"Shut up."

We had decided to have something to eat at the Turtle Kraals. It was walking distance from the marina, a couple turns off an alley named Lazy Way. A couple of bikers cruised the line of tiny shops, drawn by the smell of incense.

Babe had been laughing to herself. We ordered beer-battered shrimp and sat waterside as evening came down. There was only a little noise from the bar, and the tables near us were occupied mostly by locals who were subdued, perhaps counting the days ahead in the new year that they would waste. A handful of tourists were taking their cues from the townies. In six weeks there would be a waiting line for dinner and the dangerous grumble of too many people finding paradise all at once. We were saluting the sane weeks that remained.

"If that old fart had seen my boobies, I think I would have to kill myself," Babe said. "Honest, sugar. What happened?"

"I popped a little of this, drank a little of that." It had seemed like a fun idea, and it helped make dancing at Blackbeards' amateur strip night sound like fun, too. I half smiled, grateful I hadn't passed out in the dump. A roomful of Curtis Humphreys, each with a fantasy life that would make a crack whore check into a convent, had been throwing condoms at the stage. Someone had called Barry Irvington, who dragged me out of the place to sleep it off in his office.

"Guess an alternative would be to kill Curtis," Babe said. "That would wipe the slate clean."

"We ought to be figuring where Bennell is."

"I know. My pride is a little wounded he hasn't come back."

"That's the important thing," I said. Going through the motions, I had phoned around again, then gotten an inspiration and tried the commissioners' office at City Hall. Having come up with nothing, I was staring blankly into the middle distance, where there weren't any answers.

"Should we be worried? He *said* he was gonna see that old stinkpot."

"He may have been arrested," I said. "The feds

have two guys watching him. Trying to."

"What agency?"

"ATF."

"No kiddin'. What's your boyfriend say?"

"What?"

"The skinny cop."

"He's not my boyfriend."

"What's he say?"

"He didn't say."

"Nuthin?"

"To steer clear of them."

She chuckled. "I never met a local cop who could stand the federals, but they envy their muscle. The feeling's a little stronger down here; Uncle Sam acts like he owns South Florida."

"I could find out if Bennell's been arrested," I said.

"Call your boyfriend?"

I shook my head. "You'll have to go to the loo or take a walk."

She left without protest. Two minutes later, I had asked a favor of Gloria Hutchin, who said she would check with her friends whether Hub was in custody and call me back. Ignoring my beer, I watched lights wink on aboard nearby boats. A frail voice rose in protest at the bar, where a sports channel was on.

Sooner than I expected, my phone rang. "Hub isn't being held at the federal lockup," Gloria said. "But if I have the dirt right, ATF is displeased about the person he hired for security. Don't give them anything to use against you, Megan."

"I won't."

"I mean, stay clean. Aunt Gloria wouldn't steer you wrong. How long has Hub been missing?"

"I don't know. When you saw him this morning, did he say what he was going to do?"

"I didn't see him. He phoned about eighty-thirty. You know, I've got a feeling that Hub did something he doesn't want to answer for."

As I promised Gloria to keep her posted, Babe McKenzie slid onto the bench across from me.

"It doesn't look like he's been arrested," I said.

"So what then?"

"A friend thinks he may have run away."

"What sort of friend?" She was instantly wary. "A woman?"

"Calm down, she's twenty years older than you. If he's in a jam, he may have taken off."

"Maybe. But most guys his age who've built something know to sit tight and lawyer up. Make the other guy prove it."

"Maybe he knows they could," I said.

"And maybe we're just overreacting, and old Hubby Bear is passed out drunk at Blackbeards." She squinted hard at me. "Don't scoff, sugar. I never thought I'd hear you were there."

"Just once."

"You're never gonna live it down if I can help it."

"You got any other ideas?"

"No."

"Me either."

We ordered a pitcher of Key West Lager and sat comfortably becoming part of the night crowd. Babe asked if I had heard from my dumbass other boyfriend, and I said no. She asked if I had thought about going back to school, and I said no, which wasn't true. I thought about it twice a week. I could drink beer in New Haven, get laid by a better class of whiner, and hear the same bullshit from after-midnight philosophers. In another year I would have earned credentials for a job as an editorial assistant at a small publisher. Six months ago that had been all I wanted.

18

I parked the car in Calusa Estates and walked down to the beach. All the rooms I could see of Reena Yates's house faced the water. They all were brightly lit. Lurking on the sand for ten minutes convinced me she wasn't sharing the place with Hub Bennell. That had been the silliest possibility I could think of, but I had decided it was worth a try just because Hub had ruled it out.

I hadn't invited Babe.

It was cold on the beach. I shivered as I watched Reena Yates come into view through an archway. Holding a drink aloft, she stopped to stare through a tall window onto the beach. She had done it at the other windows, and I had caught on she was admiring her reflection. Being objective, I thought she looked pretty good for someone approaching middle age. Pretty firm, not quite lush. Not at all modest when she thought she was alone. Her skin had the luminescent whiteness of a redhead who avoids the sun. If the skin was on display every night, it was no wonder the ancient neighbor hung around on the beach.

She wandered past some side windows, then out of sight through a doorway. This was her second trip through the place since I had arrived. The ritualistic quality kept me watching. She was like a waterman's widow, or someone who wasn't sure of her status, pacing until dawn made the vigil pointless unless the drinks felled her first.

On the telephone, she had told me to go to hell. That was before I had a chance to ask if Hub was hiding out with her. The idea had grown on me after I said goodnight to Babe and picked up his car. It also struck me he wouldn't pay me anything if he didn't want to be found.

A door scraped over the sand. She stepped out of the house onto the screened patio.

"Cole?"

"Cole?"

Barely audible over the sand-scrubbing sound of the tide. When there was no answer, she teetered back inside and the door closed. She passed a window, her drink to her lips. Either the lady was bonkers or she expected her husband tonight. Both things could be true.

She climbed a few stairs and went out of sight.

A few minutes later there was an *au naturel* flicker at a distant window. I crouched and wished I had brought a heavy jacket. With the wind cutting through my clothes, I was more underdressed for my circumstances than Reena. I shivered until my teeth rattled and imagined car lights burrowing through a whiteout in New Haven. They would consider the fiftyish temperature on this beach a heat wave. Then I imagined them all sitting around log fires drinking hot cider and I shivered again.

Before long I was going to have to tackle the business of peeing on sand. I put my face down and hugged my knees. The scraping door brought my head up.

"Cole—*baby!*"

I hadn't heard a car or seen headlights.

"I've been waiting, baby!"

She was on the patio, and a man approached from the beach. A small boat was grounded fifty yards down the shore.

"Oh *Gawd* Cole baby, till you called I thought—"

Her whine cut off as he reached her. I was close enough to see a hand grab her breast and twist. She screeched.

I got up and headed for the patio. A few steps from the door, a voice behind me said, "Hey, *puta*," low and furry.

He came out of nowhere and hit me two or three times in the belly, and I doubled up and tumbled onto the sand. They dragged me inside, through the tun-

nel of plants into a bright living room. My diaphragm
was a fist-sized knot. Reena Yates was somewhere
nearby screaming.

I turned my face on the tile. If I could get my arms
to work—

Pointy black boots stepped past me, up to the
doorway to another room. My Spanish is rudimentary
but the drift was obvious. He asked whether perhaps,
if the *patron* could spare a few seconds from disciplin-
ing *la pelirroja*, he could decide what to do with this
one.

The man who came down the steps looked like the
Cole Yates I had seen on TV. Low-combed dark hair,
wide sincere eyes, black framed glasses. He was
dressed in black slacks and a black high-neck shirt.
His dark shoes looked like ballet slippers. He had the
same fluid movement that I'd seen outside Voss's
apartment and at the Sailhook marina. At a distance,
I thought, he could pass for anyone.

"Can you fuck her quickly, Che?"

For an ugly man, Che did a good imitation of a
happy face.

"Then enjoy yourself. But I do not want her dead."

He went back into the other room and cooed like a
lover to Reena Yates.

That left me with Che, of the puffy lips and pitted
skin, who had flirted with me from the lowrider outside
Voss's building. He was tall and skinny, shirtless, tattooed, with wooden beads around his neck and
pointed shoes. He did a curious ceremonial bow and

extended a hand.

"Pinky will fuck you first."

I looked the other way.

The small man must have been the one who hit me. He was muscular, pale, half-dressed in knee-length shorts and an open lavender shirt. His black hair was clipped close to the scalp. He had gold rings through his nipples. His tennis shoes had holes in the toes. His eyes were green.

Know your rapist, they say.

He bent and grabbed for the snap on my jeans. I rolled onto my side, grasping for my back. The gun was back there, under my shirt. He punched the side of my head and sat on my chest.

The scream from the other room stopped every-thing. Even our breathing stopped.

Then Che laughed nervously. "Loco bitch."

He bent and pulled my pants down to my knees.

As the smaller man levered himself up, I jabbed a fist at his crotch. The punch didn't have much behind it. He wobbled to his feet, stepped back and kicked me in the head. Twice, three times.

"I told you not to kill her."

The command from the doorway froze him.

"You take so long to fuck one Anglo?" The soft voice was mocking. "Come, *campesinos*. Help me with this one."

My eyes slitted open. The *patron* had Reena Yates by the elbow. His touch was light, as though he was steering his naked redhead out on the town.

He glanced down.

"My men wouldn't mind killing you," he said, "since you are such a bad lay."

He propelled Reena onto the patio, and the outside door scraped and the cold beach wind swept in. I tried to roll over, thinking my leaden arms could still reach the gun. Then I passed out.

I had the gun out, a round in the chamber, safety off when I went out to the beach. They had been gone for ten minutes. There was no sign of the boat that had been grounded down the shore. I thought it had been a Zodiac-like inflatable. I glimpsed the swimmer in the phosphorescent shallows near where the boat had been. Sitting in the sand, I waited until the dizziness left, then I got up, put the gun on the sand, and waded into the water. She was only a few yards out, rolling as the tide pulled her, hair fanning, breasts swaying, feet tangling, like a dancer who couldn't get over being clumsy.

I caught a hand in her hair and pulled the body in. For ten or twenty minutes I sat in the sand beside the dead woman, too exhausted and painful to move. The gigolo had cut his date's throat. Deeply and truly, romance *fini*, as the song says.

I wondered why he hadn't cut me.

I sat shivering, thinking how close Pinky had come to having it in me. Played a movie inside my head in which he was trying but I got my gun free and jammed it under his nose and pulled the trigger, spattering the room with shit. Because that's what he was.

I made sure I had the gun and walked up to the house. Inside, I found my phone and woke Barry.

19

"We will tape your ribs and you will not complain again," the young doctor said. "For your face you must have an MRI. There may be fractures. One never knows." It was four-thirty a.m., and except for me the emergency room wanted for patients. The young doctor was Asian. I let him do the taping, then told him I didn't have insurance, which ended the talk about an MRI. I got off the table, accepted a nurse's help pulling on my shirt. My face hurt worse than my side. The cheek was puffy and my left eye wasn't fully open.

"Roxicet?" he inquired.

"Definitely."

"Pick up the prescription at the desk. The police are waiting for you." He knocked the curtain aside and left.

"You don't look too good," Barry Irvington said.

I pulled my shirt together and started buttoning it. "I'm okay." A lie, I wasn't close to okay. Reena Yates's gaping white throat swam in front of my eyes. When her head tilted the wound had opened as if the bloodless lips were trying to speak.

As we left the beach two hours ago, people had been taking pictures of the body and the house. They were in no hurry. A dead person's time was spoken for.

"You said Voss's business partner was named Hoya," Barry said. "Or Avila."

He handed me a sheet of paper, a contrasty copy of an FBI poster that showed a sharp-boned, feral face.

"Look familiar?"

The face had been harshly lighted to begin with, with stark shadows deepening the eyes and cheeks. Successive reproductions had exaggerated the grainy contrasts. Not many people look their best soon after being arrested. The photograph was dated nine years earlier. The dark hair was longer. He wore a sleeveless undershirt. Small hoop earrings adorned his ears. He had put on weight since then, smoothing the narrow face, but the look of arrogance hadn't changed.

I nodded. "He looks more prosperous now."

"The hair is shorter?"

"And he doesn't wear earrings, and he dresses better some of the time."

"His name is Hector Avila, but he calls himself Paul Hoya according to this."

I read the dark print. He also had used the name Juan Castellano. The birth date on the wanted sheet made Avila thirty-eight years old, a few weeks from turning thirty-nine. Since his late teens, he had been convicted of assault, sexual battery, possession of a controlled substance, carrying a concealed weapon, and several misdemeanors. When the poster had been issued, the going charge was homicide. He had been born in Miami of Cuban-American parents. The poster suggested he might have fled to Cuba, where he had relatives. He could be working as a chauffeur, actor or musician. He had attended Dade Community College for two years (the dates were given) studying social work and theater.

"Well rounded," Barry said. "Why do you think he spared you?"

"I don't know."

"You're a witness to a murder."

I nodded.

"If my daughter brought that home—"

"You don't have a daughter."

The woman at the desk accepted my Visa card and I signed the chit, afraid to look at the total. She passed me the prescription for painkiller. We went outside to Barry's car.

"We couldn't, Laurie and I," he said. He had a shrug that classified things as inexplicable or unavoidable. "Once we were certain there wouldn't be children, staying married lost its dazzle."

He could have kept the information to himself. Wherever it led wasn't where I wanted to be with him.

"Dan sort of asked me to look after you."

"I don't need looking after."

"He said he had a good kid, but you never know about kids, do you? He worried about his health. Not the craziest conversation I ever had at Sloppy Joe's. He was going out on some job that worried him. Two weeks later, he was back in town and never mentioned it again."

It was the kind of thing he would have done, handing off a daughter like a cat he couldn't afford to keep. *Feed her once in a while.* I could believe he had gotten nervous doing the little jobs for the anonymous bastards in Washington. The list of people with good reasons for hating him had grown long over the years.

"I'll drive you home."

"Drive me back out there. I need Bennell's car."

He nodded.

I said, "Do you have a picture of Brian Voss?"

"Morgue photo."

It would do. I told him what I had in mind.

I didn't want to go home. The Carbuncle had the stale smell of exhaustion that matched my mood. Lemuel Rees was putting house quarters into the Wurlitzer. A drunken man shouting in German scribbled messages on dollar bills and stapled them to the wall to impress a Bahama Village prostitute. A serious drinker could find a dollar bill with a slogan for every occasion.

Lem drifted to the bar. In an hour it would be dawn and he would be pulling pints of bait fish out of the cooler to go with the six packs he sold to boaters.

"What's your wish, ma'am?"

"Diet ginger ale," I said. My face was turned away from him. I'd pulled my hair loose and let it hang across my squinty eye like the old movie star did.

"Where's Timbo?"

"Belize." Why not tell everyone.

"Belize? Without you?" He considered. "I heard people talking about Belize. There's supposed to be whole hillsides of weed for sale. Amazing, huh?"

"Incredible." My face ached worse when I spoke.

"So you're looking for someone to keep you company." The scraggly beard split as he savored the moment. "I could ask around."

"You could get hurt."

"Remember the offer."

"I've had enough offers tonight."

"You don't look like you feel so hot."

Beneath the scuz, here was an observant, caring guy. The thought made me laugh, which really hurt. The drug stores wouldn't be open for hours, except for the one Lem ran from under the counter.

"There's one kind of business we can do," I said. "What are you selling?"

"We're not that good friends." He raised his hands. "I guess we *could* be, depending how hard up you are."

I thought about shooting him. An act of public hygiene.

In the end I settled for a double shot of whiskey and a bag of ice and stumbled across the road to the boat.

20

They came aboard an hour after dawn and introduced themselves. Ernie White and Randy Nash,
agents for the U.S. Bureau of Alcohol, Tobacco and
Firearms.

"Man, this place smells bad."

I raised my head from the pillow. Neither man had
drawn a gun. The young guy stood in the salon,
bending under the low ceiling and sniffing. Behind
him a man with lean tan arms rested against the steps
from the deck. I hadn't bothered locking up. Had
crashed onto the bed still in my clothes. I rubbed my
eyes and looked at my watch. The hands said I had
gotten two hours sleep.

"Do you have a no-knock warrant?"

"We knocked." Randy Nash's short black hair was

brushed straight back; dampness or perhaps mousse had spiked it like the checking on a pistol grip. His round face looked soft the way boys who injure small-er boys can look soft. The hazel eyes were widely spaced, the mouth small. A white knit shirt hugged his biceps. A badge hung from a belt loop on his jeans.

He opened a cupboard over the port side bunk and began dumping things onto the cushion, dirty clothes, paperback books, a moldy sail bag. When he smiled while looking inside the sail bag, I got a bad feeling. If he had it in for me, he could have come aboard earlier and planted something.

"Where do you keep your gun?"

"Behind you, on the shelf."

I throw everything onto the railed shelf, sunglasses, phone, keys, money, Walther in its holster. He pulled the gun, pushed the button that dropped the maga-zine, then worked the slide and handed the weapon to his partner.

"Fired?" Randy asked.

"No way. She doesn't clean it."

"Doesn't clean anything. If my wife was this big a pig, I'd send her home to that uncle who was so friendly." Holding a pen, he poked through my clothes, lifted a pair of black underpants that had a hole in the butt. Shaking his head, he let them fall.

I said something.

Nash looked around. "What was that?"

"That does it."

He grinned. "You hear that? She says 'That does it.' I'm in trouble now, pardner."

"There goes your pension."

"Would you really fuck with my pension, sis?"

"Till it couldn't walk."

He chuckled. "Tell us why you visited the medical examiner's office during the examination of Brian Voss."

I stopped rubbing my face. "Get out of here unless you've got a warrant."

They didn't.

"Dr. Lewis said you were interested in the condition of the slug. Care to explain why?"

"I wanted to know if the person I was guarding had shot Voss," I said.

"Did he?"

"It wasn't conclusive. He might have winged him. He didn't put the small-caliber slug in his head."

"And you were nosing around up in Lauderdale for the same reason?"

"Pretty much."

He was playing with things in another cupboard, his back mostly turned to me. His partner, who had squeezed into the salon, joined the hunt for buttons and bottle caps. It was a relaxed search. I got ready for the hilarity if they opened the drawer that held condoms and K-Y.

Without looking around, Nash said, "I say we take her in, Ern. That old colored lady really gets off doing cavity searches."

White leaned on a corner in the dining nook, his weathered face pinched into a sincere look. "We're just trying to figure out where we can find Commissioner Bennell."

"I don't know," I said.

"We've covered some of the same ground as you," White said. "Without getting into confidential details, we think Bennell may have been a bad boy. You don't want to get between us and him."

"I wish I could help."

"You know, I believe you mean it," White said. "What happened to your face?"

They hadn't heard about Reena Yates or we would be dancing a different jig.

"She hangs out in rough bars," Nash said.

I was silent and White lost interest. "Let's hit the road," he said. "Unless she's got more underpants?"

"I'll catch up," said Nash as the older man climbed the steps to the deck. Nash hooked his thumbs in his belt loops. With his back arched, it was a no-hands peeing stance. "Did your old man ever tell you about me?"

"Not that I remember."

"I'm the badass that was trying to put him in jail."

"I'm sure he didn't mention you." That was the cruelest thing I could think of to say.

"He figured that because he worked for some spooks, he could shit on my turf. Big mistake."

"I guess it's too late to tell him that."

"If he wasn't dead, he'd be doing hard time. He

was pretty old for that. But you're not." There was substantial intelligence in his glance. "I sent a guy up once for breathing hard on a woman I was chasing. When the staties pulled a kilo of flake out of the guy's Buick, you should have seen his face. He was realizing, just like that, that his life was over."

The intense, slightly wild look in Nash's eyes convinced me he was telling the truth. He was reliving one of his happier moments.

He climbed out of the cabin. When I felt the boat rock, I got up, went to a window and watched as they walked down the catwalk. When they heard about Reena Yates they would be back, unless they found a real lead to investigate. I didn't think I should count on that.

I left the hatch open so the breeze could dilute the stink of cologne one of them wore. It was strong and peppery, made for guys who wanted to smell like alligator wrestlers.

I put away some of the stuff Nash had disturbed. On the railed shelf was a picture he had contemplated while deciding how bad he wanted to scare me. It had to have been taken ten years ago, because when I was twelve or so I had thought bobs were tremendously mature. Dad didn't look much different. The shaggy hair might have had more black in it. The long hollow cheeks made the face look, at that particular moment, ascetic. We were both at the wheel of the *KeyHole* with royal palms towering in the background, and I realized Mom had taken this picture after delivering me somewhere near Miami to the ex-husband she pitied but still trusted with their only child. A day of high clouds and green water during spring break or summer vacation. We must have had a good time. Nobody had fallen overboard.

Staring at the picture, I couldn't figure out why good times were over before you knew it. The lousy stuff stuck around. I could still smell the jerk's cologne.

21

I had tossed the knapsack that held my last clean clothes into the back of the convertible, my getaway almost complete, when Barry drove into the marina yard and climbed out of his car. He was dragging around the same baggy suit from last night and hadn't shaved. Walking past me, drinking from a paper cup, he looked over my boat.

"Is the crock seaworthy?"

The fiberglass hull, despite a couple of blisters in the gelcoat, was seaworthy if the sea was flat and the air was gentle. She was afloat.

"I haven't taken it out," I said.

"Why not?"

I hadn't thought of anywhere to go.

"Curtis Humphrey sleeps at the harbor master's office," Barry said. "An hour ago he identified photos of Voss and Avila. Humphrey is pretty certain they were the men bringing boats through the marina. Why did you think they might be doing that?"

"I was guessing."

"If I hired your boat for the morning, would we sink a hundred feet from the dock?"

"Probably not."

He bought fuel at Hawkes's pump, and when we cleared the marina into the Atlantic, on the protected side of the reef, I coaxed the inboard engine up to six knots and turned the wheel over to Barry. The cracked rib hurt so bad I was sweating and nauseated. He had found binoculars below and shed his jacket and tie and rolled up the sleeves of his shirt. Cutting the throttle, he leaned on the curved roof of the cabin and focused the binoculars on the shore.

"What are we looking for?" I said.

"Hector Avila's boat."

"The Zodiac?" I tried to prop myself at an angle that didn't hurt.

"Something bigger. Twice that you know of, he's come and gone by boat. He needs a base, and a boat would give him flexibility. You didn't actually see him driving a car up at Sailhook. He could have come in by water."

In that case he hadn't followed me there.

As we passed the small yacht basins along Cow Key Channel, I wondered how Barry expected to know which boat Avila occupied, if any, among the thousands in the Lower Keys. I took stock of him. He was getting too much whiskey and not enough sleep. There was nothing I could do about that. I didn't want to take his wife's place, or his mother's—or, when you came down to it, the place of the daughter he didn't have.

We spent ninety minutes checking boats at Safe Harbor and Oceanside. Thousands of boats. Thousands of places to hide a boat. If Avila was afloat, he could be tied up at Bennell's house and we wouldn't know unless we checked there. As we followed Boca Chica Channel under the highway into the smoother water of the Gulf of Mexico, a jet screamed overhead. A Naval Air Station occupied most of Boca Chica Key, and pilots were practicing landings, tapping wheels onto the runway and leaping back into the air. Somehow I knew the maneuver was called "touch and go." I had probably picked up the phrase watching the exercise from a leaky sailboat when I was too young to remember. That long ago, Mom might have been with us. I got up and looked at the chart flapping above the wheel. Barry had lined us up with Monday Key on the starboard side, Bush Key on the port. Neither low-lying clump of sand seemed worth naming. The little island on the right could have been called Tuesday without raising an argument for or against Monday, and Bush Key was almost barren.

A few fishing boats were getting a late start, backlit shadows pushing out onto the Gulf ahead of dark creases of wake. A golf course slid past on our right, bordered by massive townhouses that both dwarfed the intermittent mangrove and made the natural setting look cheap and phony.

He was steering us closer to land.

"Do you know who runs Sailhook?" Barry asked. "It's a family business, owned by two Folger daughters, both old maids. Jim Riggs, who isn't family, is general manager."

We were past the golf course, past the mansions. He was searching for something.

The channel he found looked at first like a shadow thrown by the mangrove. It was about fifty feet wide. Once we passed the screen of trees, the water opened up into a small harbor occupied by a marina and a boat repair yard. There was a large, well-maintained pier, to which several pontoon boats were tethered. Placards on the boats offered sunset cruises and snorkeling.

About twenty other boats were tied at slips connected to the main pier by wooden walkways. Not many people were out. A woman in tennis whites was jogging along the big pier. On the aft deck of a small boat, a boy was unlashing a mainsail cover. We drifted toward the docks. A sign atop a shotgun-style shack of weathered board identified the place as Sailhook Dive Center.

"The Folger girls own three marinas," Barry said. "You know the big one in Marathon. There's also a small operation in Largo and this place." Barry leaned over and fended off as we reached the pier. He dropped a bumper into the gap between the pier and the hull, went forward and put another bumper over the side as I cut the engine.

Climbing onto the roof, I looked at the cruisers that were within view. It's hard to tell one make from another if you're not an owner. Next door, a big Hatteras, sporting the familiar extended deckhouse, was a picture of domesticity with laundry hung outside the cabin. Except for what I'd already seen, there was nobody stirring. I couldn't see much farther down the line.

"Any candidates?"

"None with Zodiacs in plain sight," I said.

As we climbed ashore, a small, copper-skinned man came out of the office waving a clipboard. "No docking!" he called.

When Barry showed his badge, the man ran back into the shack. The door slammed.

"He thinks I'm *la migra*," Barry said. He approached the building, avoiding the windows, and called, *"No ser la migra!"*

The only response was a shout behind us. "Hey, folks!" A man stood on the deck of a nearby sailboat grinning around big dentures. He was barrel-chested, bald, with lizard-dark skin, yellow eyebrows, white chest hair. His only clothing was a string bikini.

"I'll be sorry to see the Sanchezes go," he called. "Mama cooks a mean *mole poblano*."

"Help me out and she can have citizenship," Barry said. "Does anyone here have a Zodiac on board?"

The old man's grin was frozen, as if he had been planning to pee over the side until we came along. Hard little marble eyes, sunk deep, admitted he wanted to be doing something. "The fellows in slip fourteen had something like that."

Barry looked up the line of boats. The old man said, "Slip fourteen's the one next to me. You can see it's empty. They must have left during the night, but I didn't hear it. Until I put the Beltone in, you could blow the boat up under me and I wouldn't hear."

"What about since you put it in?"

"Quiet, till you two showed up." He bent and touched his knuckles to the deck. "Good morning for a run, I'd say. Don't tell Senora Sanchez, but I don't like every Latino I meet. This bunch was driving a boat way too big for their pedigree."

"What kind of boat was it?" Barry said.

"Expensive. They didn't get it washing dishes."

"Do you know the make?"

"Power boats don't interest me. They're too big and they stink like smudge pots. Your little sloop is my speed. First time I ever saw an immigration cop arrive under sail."

"What about the boat's name?" I said.

"Never gave it a glance. *La Mordida* would be about right. Nasty bunch."

"Mexican?" *Mordida* was a word I associated with Mexico.

"Mex, Cuban, Honduran, Salvadoran—who can tell? The boss could act white when he wanted. The other day he left here wearing a blue blazer looking just a little suntanned."

"How many people were on board?" Barry said.

"Three or four. I didn't get too nosy."

"How long were they here?"

"Three nights? What've you got on them?"

We heard the door opening and saw Senor Sanchez nod from the doorway. He went inside and we followed. A large moon-faced woman sat dejectedly on a sofa beneath a mounted carcass of a sand shark.

Barry went behind the counter and found the marina registry book. "Slip fourteen was rented to an Island Packet named *Elsinore*."

"Island Packet would be a sailboat," I said.

He ran a finger along other entries. "What kind of boat was in slip fourteen, Mr. Sanchez?"

The man traded a glance with the woman. "Senor Jim took care of that," he said.

"Jim Riggs? What sort of boat, Mr. Sanchez?"

"A Chris Craft."

"How big was it?"

"Forty-five feet."

"Did it have a name?"

"Yes, sir. *Morning Glory*."

"Where do I find Jim Riggs?"

He led us outside, pointed through the scrubby pine behind the shack. A pickup truck was bouncing along an unpaved road toward the boat repair yard.

The water curved around that way, past the marina

slips. We walked down the pier into the yard. Twenty feet from the inlet, a big cabin cruiser was up on blocks. Nearby, two men were setting up to work on the patched bottom of a smaller sportfisher. One man was stirring a five-gallon bucket while the other picked at the nap of a roller. The nearer man had stringy blond hair leaking from a bandanna, narrow shoulders, and sponge sweatbands on his wrists. The lighted end of a cheroot bobbed above the paint roller.

He became aware of me watching and decided the best idea was to ignore the intrusion. The other man, who was bent over the paint bucket, had a close-shaven head, an eyebrow ring, tattoos on both bare shoulders. He noticed Barry, who in rumpled slacks with a holstered gun was hard to mistake for anything but a cop.

Barry walked over to them. "And what are your names?"

"Rodney Parson, boss."

"John Parson."

"Okay, boys, sit down and cross your ankles. Either of you carrying a weapon?"

"Just my pocket knife," the blond man said.

"Leave it in your pocket. What about you?"

"Nuthin."

"On parole?"

"Yes, sir. Nine more months."

"How long have you been out?"

"Eight days and almost fourteen hours."

"This boat belong to you?"

"Can't afford no boat."

"What do you spend all your money on?"

The blond man answered. "Mr. Jim don't pay much, so I spend mine on weed. John don't. He's gotta stay clean for nine months."

"That's a long time," Barry said. "So you fellas are brothers."

"No sir." The dark-haired one spoke. "We're married. Six days, almost six hours."

Stepping past them, Barry inspected the larger boat. It was a nice fat hulk with a flybridge and the strong smell of fresh-cut wood and varnish. The bridge looked too new to have been out to sea. I followed Barry toward the stern. The craft's name, numbers and manufacturer's plate had been removed.

He called to the Parsons. "Who steals the boats?"

"Dunno, officer. I just started yesterday."

"Pretty dumb employment for a guy on parole. What about you, Rodney?"

"I don't know where the boats come from. But I've seen things that might be worth a deal. For John and me."

"Like what?"

"I've seen the guy Mr. Jim takes orders from. Fact, he was here yesterday. Mr. Jim calls him Hector."

"Am I under arrest?" the man on parole said.

"Right now we'll call it custody," Barry said, hunkering beside them. "What else do you know?"

22

They brought Jim Riggs to the station that afternoon. He was bald across the top but had sparse ginger fuzz growing above his ears and on his arms. He wore cotton ducks and a green knit shirt on the left breast of which the Sailhook logo arched smartly like a jumping fish. His expression varied from bored to angry. He had sat in the interview room for more than an hour without anyone looking in on him except through the one-way glass.

Barry opened the door and said regretfully, "The Parson boys gave you up."

Barry stepped inside, and I followed and closed the door. Barry had told me how we would do it.

Riggs's voice was deep. "I asked for a lawyer more than an hour ago."

As if he hadn't heard, Barry said, "How long have you been fixing up stolen boats?"

"I don't know anything about stolen boats." Hunching over the table, he let the silence stretch half a minute before tilting his head at me. "What's she doing here?"

"She's here so she can testify you never asked for a lawyer."

"You son of a bitch."

Barry shrugged. "Your workers traded their asses for yours. The Sanchezes are talking to an interpreter. I don't care much whether you help yourself or not. Are the Folger women in on it?"

Squinting, Riggs said, "So what if I do cosmetic work for a few customers?"

"If you do it for people who steal boats, it's a chop shop. Missy, did Mr. Riggs ask for a lawyer?"

I shook my head.

"Waived, didn't he?"

"Yes, he did."

Riggs's face reddened. "What's she, some hooker you got a case on?"

"Missy is an undercover agent for the U.S. Customs Service," Barry said. "Between us we've got an airtight case on you. I'm surprised you were dumb enough to do business with a guy like Avila."

Barry slid the high-contrast picture of Hector Avila, with a ring in his ear and hair to his shoulders, in front of Riggs.

"I wish I'd never heard of the bastard," Riggs said.

***

It was like this. For three years, Jim Riggs had re-habbed stolen boats when normal repair business was slack. The slack time was reliably seasonal. It happened to fall during the same summer months when large numbers of expensive boats sat idle at swank berths in South Florida. In less than a week, for not much money, Riggs's yard could change the profile, visible electronics and identification of million-dollar yachts on their way from Fort Lauderdale to un-discriminating buyers in South America. For Riggs and a boat thief named Ashley Scottle in Miami, it amounted to low-risk entrepreneurship. Scottle sold marine insurance. Between June and August, hun-dreds of yachts wore signs that said STEAL ME to Scottle's alert eye. They had a window of a few days, sometimes months, before a boat's absence from its pier was noticed. More than enough time for a run down to an obscure boat yard in the Keys. Two heists a summer kept the men comfortable.

Hector Avila took over the Miami end of the busi-ness from Ashley Scottle a year ago.

"Made it plain he'd done Ashley. Liked making it plain," Riggs said.

Avila and his partner Brian brought down the boats, and it became a year-round business. Riggs didn't like to think about how some of the yachts were ac-quired. A new Seastar arrived with the master state-room ribboned with week-old blood. On top of which,

Riggs found he was performing the work for pretty much cost and getting no share of the profits. He had become hired labor.

"Last June I had this mouthy black kid working for me. Pain in the ass, talked all the time but I sort of liked him. Bebe knew he was funny. We were replacing the railing on the Seastar when Avila came by to hurry the work up. The kid was in good form. He started saying stuff about Cubans, how they don't look all that white. With those big lips you know it ain't just suntans they all got. Avila nods. The African taint explains a lot about his homeland, he says. But himself he's pure Castilian. That's someone from Spain. Bebe says the sun must shine awful hard in Spain."

Avila came up on deck while he talked about being purebred Spanish. He talked nice and soft, like a school teacher who wanted you to learn.

"I didn't see the knife till he'd opened Bebe's belly. The kid's holding his guts in, and Avila sits in a fishing chair talking about Spanish culture."

"What became of Bebe?"

"What do you think?"

"Where did you get rid of the body?"

"I didn't. The psycho wouldn't have trusted me with it. His guy Fuentes cleaned up the mess. They'd come in a cigarette boat all whored up for racing, and they left with the kid rolled up in newspapers. I figured Hector was going to kill me sooner or later. But he just kept bringing the boats through like nothing had happened. There was one in August, maybe, what's that, five months ago, and that was the end of it. That was the last time I saw him until this week."

"Whose boats are in the yard now?"

"Word got around, you know. There's a crew up in Boca who've been moving some stuff down the waterway. Truth is, I was thinking of closing down the business. I knew sooner or later one of the bums I hired would start talking."

"Do you know what changed after August?"

"I hoped Hector'd got killed. Thought a few times about dropping a dime on him—except Fuentes or one of the others would still be loose."

I butted in. "Describe Fuentes."

He described a small bull who could have been Pinky.

Barry seemed not to hear. He stared at Riggs. "Was there anything different in August?"

"Couple of other guys showed up with the regulars who brought the boats. And a woman. Better class of skunks."

"Did you get their names?"

"One was Carlos something."

"Who were the regulars?"

"Avila, his buddy Brian. Usually Fuentes and a creep named Che."

"What was the last boat?"

"Fifty-three-foot Hatteras, twenty years old. Not really worth stealing."

"What was it called?"

139

"When it came into the yard, right around the end of July, it was *Barbara Bell*, out of Vero Beach. When it left, it was *Two Earls*, out of Newport News. He didn't care what we called them. He understood what we had to do."

"What was that?"

"You can't just slap on a name and numbers. The Coast Guard's all computerized. You have to borrow the identity of another boat, a sister ship that hasn't been stolen. That's what we did. If the Coast Guard ever made a full inspection, we were fucked because the papers wouldn't be right. But you don't give the Coast Guard a reason to board."

"Was there anything special about the *Two Earls*?"

"Nondescript—not high-end enough you'd look twice. Avila wanted the flying bridge taken down, so I did that, a few other things. Ashley and me went for classier ships. We didn't want some hundred footer that everyone would be looking for, but we went for boats that were worth our trouble. You put twenty thousand into fixing it up, you wanted to get a few hundred for it. With Avila, sometimes he brought in something worth selling; other times"—Riggs shrugged—"it was like he had other plans."

"What's he got now?"

"An old Chris Craft. Didn't want any work done. Just a slip for a week."

"How many people were with him?"

"Just Fuentes and Che that I saw. They scared the crap out of the Sanchezes."

"What is the boat's name?"

"*Morning Glory.* Isn't that some name for a boat?"

"Describe it."

"Like I said, a Chris Craft, older, forty-five foot Commander, you don't see many around anymore."

Barry was slumped against the wall, hands in his pockets, staring at the ceiling as if Riggs didn't really interest him. "Was Cole Yates involved in your business?"

"The mayor? Hell, no."

"I heard some of Avila's boats stopped at the city marina."

"That don't make sense. You got a boat where the papers aren't perfect, you want to move it out fast. Brokers down in the Leewards handle the next step. Another name change, new papers. I heard you can get it done in Mexico, too. But who trusts Mexicans?"

"Who was Avila dealing with?"

Riggs shook his head. "The schizo never confided in me. But that guy Carlos, now that I think about it, he could have been Mexican. Had Indian blood, you could see it, like the Sanchezes, but with money. Put on like he was a gentleman."

We went outside.

"They shut down in August," I said. "That was about the time Curtis Humphrey noticed the boats."

"It was about the time a lot of things happened," Barry said. "Yates disappeared. Your father—"

"Did you suspect Riggs before we went to Sailhook this morning?"

"No. I was guessing Sailhook was Avila's comfort zone. I'll have Terrence drive you back to your boat."

23

In the late afternoon, I drove out to Bennell's Air Charter. It was almost hot, and I parked in the shade of
the office. Steve Taylor was locking the doors to the
boathouse where the planes were hangared.

On the phone he had introduced himself as if I
wouldn't remember him—Mr. Bennell's pilot, Steve
Taylor, no relation to Fort Zachary Taylor. I had been
too tired to say hah-hah.

"Found your phone number in the office," he said.
"You don't mind me calling, do you?"

I realized too late that my sunglasses were hanging
from my collar. He took in my bruised eye but didn't
comment. He was so serious-looking he couldn't be
much fun.

"I don't mind," I said.

"Do you know where the boss is?" he said. Without waiting for an answer he gestured toward the office and we went inside.

"I don't mind waiting to get paid, and Luis and his family feel the same," he said. "But Mr. Bennell signs the fuel invoices and writes the checks. Someone from the newspaper called asking if we wanted to continue our ad. I didn't know the answer. Sometimes Mr. Bennell stops the ads for a while. Point is, someone needs to make decisions."

"Do you know what needs doing?"

"It's not like a lot of bills have piled up. There's nothing urgent about bills anyway, is there? No one cuts the telephone off if you're a week late."

He seemed to recognize me as an expert on late payments.

"But we need fuel. We use a lot of that."

"Who is Bennell's regular lawyer?"

He gave me a blank stare. "Regular?"

Hub had hired Woody Erskine in case he was in trouble for the shooting. If the pilot didn't know about that, it wasn't my business to tell him. Doubting Erskine bothered with routine stuff, I said, "There's got to be somebody handling licenses, that sort of thing."

We rooted through his boss's littered desk until Steve found a stack of business cards held together by a rubber band. We divided the stack and sorted through the cards, and he came up with the only lawyer, J. Beauregard Parker, Counselor at Law, on Duval Street. On the telephone, Parker sounded ancient as he ordered me to call him "Beau." I explained things, and he asked how long Bennell had been missing.

"A day or so."

He said, "*That* long?" chuckling. "Best thing for you children to do is pay the bills for Hubbard— routine stuff, mind you—and keep a record and if he don't show up in seven years, we'll get him declared dead and the estate will kindly reimburse you."

A funny man.

Palm over the receiver, I consulted with the pilot.

"Mr. Parker? Beau. Here's the problem, sir. If the two pilots and I pooled our available cash, we could just about pay for one day's ad in the *Citizen*."

"God's sake, all I hear from is poor people. Can you at least bring the papers to my office? If you find a check book, bring that. We'll put it under lock and key."

"Thanks," I said.

"Thanks don't buy tequila."

We collected the company check book, locked the office, and I drove us down to Duval Street. Steve Taylor climbed out of the car in front of a building that had once been a palatial movie theater with columns lifting the marquee a story and a half above the street. T-shirts filled the first floor windows, and Beauregard Parker had an office upstairs. I didn't want to go up for fear the old lawyer would demand the keys to the BMW.

"Wait a minute," I said before Steve Taylor turned

away. "I wanted to show you and Luis this." I handed him a copy Barry had given me of the police photographs of Voss and Avila and waited while he frowned.

"Am I supposed to recognize them?" he said.

"Do you?"

He hesitated, then pointed. "The one with long hair could be Luis's mother."

"Thanks a lot."

He leaned on the door. "Have you ever been to Fort Jefferson?"

"Years ago," I said, and he looked at me with surprise and approval. I added, "Before I lived here."

"Oh, sure," he said understanding. "If we come up one customer short on a flight, would you like to tag along? Special rate for working crew. You can point out the wrecks while I fly."

He handed back the photocopy.

"That's possible," I said.

"Good."

Driving off I felt almost cheerful. I liked his way of going at things. He made an offer without too much explanation, and you took it or left it. Moses was on his corner, arms raised as if waiting for the rapture, tongue abusing tourists who thought a robed madman was quaint. Two fingers clutched one of his blunts, and its fragrance gave me a five-second high as I drove past. Piers-Paul, the town's best mime, was in front of his usual restaurant wearing white-face paint and holding aloft a board listing dinner specials.

Just inside the city marina's gate I parked illegally, put on my sunglasses, and went looking for Curtis Humphrey. He was out on his evening rounds. The breeze kept shifting and he stank whichever way it blew. I was wearing a sleeveless sweatshirt and jeans so he ignored my chest.

"Look at this!" he cried. "Doctor goes to college ten years learning to cut brains like sausage and he can't park an effing boat."

The cruiser that offended him was twice as long as the *KeyHole*, with a teak rear deck cluttered with twin jet skis and a canopied dining area at midships where a small table was laid with stemware and china I knew I couldn't have paid for. The name on the transom, instead of hinting at the good gleanings from surgery, was *Marbella*. To me the boat appeared to be properly docked, but I didn't say this to Curtis. He stood scratching his neck as he blinked angrily.

I reminded him why I was there. "The last time you saw the men with the boats, was anyone new with them?"

"Lady, what can a half-blind drunk remember from last summer?" His mostly toothless mouth chewed itself. "This fool should park the effing boat out in the shipping lanes."

"It could be important."

"Will you dance at Blackbeards again?"

"No chance."

"You were cute without your clothes on."

"Curtis, do you want me to kill you?"

"Don't much care. A gentleman can ask, can't he? If you want to see the docking records for the last time those fellows were here, I suppose I could show them to you."

"You've got a record?"

"I thought there was something odd about those two. It's in the office."

His smell filled every corner of the small building.

"We only log the overnighters and the cruise ships. Sometimes I forget to do that. But I made sure I put down everything about these boys." Scabby fingers roamed across a keyboard. Looking over his shoulder I watched names roll down the screen. "There you go, fourth of August, fifty-three foot Hatteras, stayed one night, left before dawn on the fifth. *Two Earls*, showing Newport News as home port. There's the Coast Guard registration number."

"You said before it wasn't much of a boat."

"Did I?" He rolled his eyes. "It had alterations to the superstructure that were not well-considered in my opinion."

"What sort?"

"Some jackass had removed the flybridge. Made it look like a dumpy old tub."

"Did the registration number check out?"

"Sure did. So that was that. Nobody cares, I can't make 'em care. And if I stirred things up too much, the city could probably find some other rummy to fill this job."

"Was anyone else on board?"

"I didn't see anyone, but I wasn't sittin' in the office with a spyglass." He gave a sly grin. "I got warned about that. We get a lot of famous people through here, and they like you to mind your own beeswax."

"Like Cher?"

"Probably not her. The mayor told me if I got caught peeping at the ladies, he'd can me regardless of his father."

I tried to sort that out. "Who's the mayor's father?"

"He's how I got this job. One Eye Tom Yates. Couldn't shoot worth a damn. Spent a month up on the Yalu River, and Tom never hit anything except by accident. He was the mayor's dad, saw his old Army buddy was down on his luck—that's when I showed up piss broke on his doorstep—and made the boy put me on the city payroll." His smile faded. "That was timely, because Tom crossed the river himself a few weeks later."

"The Yalu?"

"The Styx. It's a good thing you're cute, honey, because you surely don't know much about the world."

"But you had to mind your own business."

"That's never a bad thing for a man to do."

"Is that why you took your suspicions about the boats to Commissioner Bennell instead of the mayor?"

"The girl wins the prize." He pulled out a half-pint of gin and offered the bottle to me.

"No thanks."

I took myself outside. If Bennell had passed the

word to Avila, Curtis was lucky he hadn't ended up on the bottom of the harbor. The dates in his records interested me. The Hatteras called *Two Earls* had left the marina on August 5. My father's boat had been found adrift two days later.

When I called J. Beauregard Parker's office, he said Mr. Taylor had left and the phone went click. He had spent enough time on young people without money.

I drove a few blocks and found an empty bar stool at Pepe's. Ginger ale covers only so many situations. I ordered a beer and imagined myself in fifty years smelling pissy and talking with phony eloquence as I reminded the young men I'd gone to Yale, yessiree, lads, so give Granny Megs a bounce, eh?

For some reason, I laughed. A bearded guy who hadn't heard the joke looked at me.

I focused on my itty bitty coincidence.

Had he been on a job? He had told both Mom and me that he had definitely, completely retired. He had ducked the last assignments the turds briefcased down from Virginia. He had promised.

But he had always been a lying son of a bitch, it went with the job.

I looked around. The bearded guy was kidding the bartender, who was a muscular blond six-footer. There was no chance either of them had visited

Blackbeards. I was the siren luring Curtis and Lemuel. And an artist bum, but not enough that he had stayed.

The bartender and the customer were admiring each other. It's a misconception that gay men all have confidential women friends. The busy studs don't have time for girl-to-girl dissing of Liza's surgery. The hunt consumes them. Just as I was telling myself how utterly useless they were, the bartender came over and said, "Megan, you look unhappy. You need a Friday night out busting up bars—not this one please—and Russell has offered to escort you."

Russell was giving a neutral grin that told me only that the bartender had set us up and he didn't mind.

"Tell Russell thanks," I said, "but I'm working. Tell yourself thanks, too."

"*Por nada*. Unhappy customers are bad for business, unless they consume excessively. Want another?"

I shook my head. Removed myself from Pepe's stool. Went out to the car and turned on the headlights as dusk settled in.

24

Gloria Hutchin was alone on her patio. She had dressed for a party in a deep green gown that shimmered with reflections of her coppery hair. Her legs were crossed; a hand cupped upward on her knee supported a cordial glass. Torches burned around the pool. The cottages where her hangers-on lived were dark.

"Come on, come on!" she called out. "I would sooner talk to you than go to the Stones' shindig. That's not a backhanded compliment. They put together a first rate group of nearly literate drunks."

"Thank you for waiting," I said.

"Don't thank me. Come sit next to me."

There wasn't much room for a second person on the cast iron love seat. As I squeezed in and our thighs brushed, she reached to a table behind us and handed me a glass brimming with sherry. She lifted her own glass a few inches. "To whatever tomorrow brings."

I took a sip, asked my question.

"Was my father still working for the Agency when he died?"

Her silence didn't last long. "He wouldn't have told anyone, of course. Does something make you think he was on an assignment?"

"There's a coincidence." I brought her up to date, told her about Hector Avila, the timing of the refitted Hatteras's departure.

"Do you know what the boat was doing?"

"No. Something illegal."

"Involving Dan?"

"I don't know."

She lifted her glass now and then. "I'm out of date, Megan, but you know who I worked for. They're bastards, each and every one of them, ours as well as theirs. The Cubans almost killed your father. You know that, don't you? You would have been just a baby, but he was in the field anyway. They held him at the Isla de Pinos prison. They injected gasoline in his joints and beat him so badly he couldn't walk. When he escaped, the people at Langley treated him like a leper for years. They couldn't be sure he hadn't been turned. Then they needed someone crazy for a mission and Dan got himself back on their A list. Total shits, all of them. To answer your question, I don't think he was still working for them."

I nodded.

"But he wouldn't have told me," Gloria said. "I've been out of action too long for that kind of trust. Dan and I talked a lot about the past, because that was what we had in common. The present—well, he was an alcoholic and I had made a good life for myself." She was silent for a few seconds. A tear glided down her cheek and she brushed at it. "The last time the Agency sent one of their people to visit me was twenty years ago. I was in Virginia with my mother, trying to put Gloria back together—at least to the point where she could go on living. I told the light colonel who drove down I would kill the next person they sent."

She scooped up the bottle, and we went inside. The kitchen was at the back of the house. She filled our glasses.

"Did Dad ever mention having trouble with two ATF agents?"

"I know they didn't like him."

"Do you know why?"

"Dan believed he had a free hand when he was on a job. That drives law enforcement people crazy. Especially," she smiled, "when they can't be sure whether he's on an official job or one of his own."

"Did he do that?"

"We all did, dear. The bastards didn't give us much in the way of retirement plans."

I showed her my pictures of Voss and Avila. She

shook her head. "After Aunt Gloria's time, but they look the part. This one's a morgue photo, isn't it? The man Hubbard shot? The other boy looks—nasty."

"He is. He has two helpers." I didn't describe their effort at rape. "One is named Fuentes and goes by 'Pinky.' The other calls himself 'Che.'"

"Che?" She laughed harshly. "I didn't think the name was popular off college campuses. It tells you who his heroes are."

"Che Guevara?" I could prove I had been on a college campus.

"Would you believe he was a medical doctor? Somehow they're always the most bloodthirsty."

"Avila or one of his men cut Reena Yates's throat."

"Do you know why?"

"She didn't have what he wanted."

"And what was that?"

"Something to do with a boat?"

"Back to that."

I nodded. "Maybe. It could be something else."

"What about Hubbard?"

"Avila was looking for him."

She sighed. "Perhaps I'll skip tonight's party."

"Hub may be okay," I said. "Avila may not have found him."

"I'm too old to be kidded, Megan."

Setting down my glass, I said, "I'd better be going."

"Be a good girl and let yourself out. Damn it to hell. I was so planning to be cheerful tonight."

***

Stopping at a copy shop, I ran off another generation of mugs, slipped a copy under Babe McKenzie's door.

I drove across the island to Hawkes Marina and locked the car. The marina was half empty. My boat had been ransacked.

The hungry and downtrodden from Bahama Village were the usual suspects, but they seldom bothered. Castaways from up north were less discriminating. Tonight was different. A methodical search had torn apart the boat from one end to the other. There was no sign of malice, nothing broken out of frustration. They had just been very thorough. Covers slit from foam cushions, drawers broken free of their stops so the backs could be inspected. Plenty of damage without any bad feelings.

The federals had come and gone. Dope heads lacked such discipline. So I supposed that left Avila.

They hadn't gotten as far as pulling the walls and ceiling apart. The spare gun was still in its ceiling compartment. I left it there and closed the panel. The photographs of my father and me were gone. So were our letters.

I sat in the darkness of the cockpit and held the old rubber-clad binoculars and took a good long look around the marina. Nothing seemed out of order. There were no big vessels I didn't recognize. Nothing of more than forty feet in any case. No Chris Craft.

He had his Zodiac, and he could have the *Morning*

Glory anchored a mile out past the reef. Even with the Coast Guard looking, he might be that brazen.

With the family photographs and letters gone, I no longer believed in coincidence. Avila's business and my father's had converged somewhere. Avila had known it before I did. Hadn't cut my throat— gentleman that he was—because I still might give him what Bennell and Reena hadn't.

25

We hit another air pocket and dropped as if someone had cut the elevator's cables. My head was tilted back, eyes closed, flesh clammy. I had never liked flying. I had turned down the pilot's offer of a wad of chewing gum. Now I wished I had accepted.

"You need a cup?" Steve Taylor said.

As I shook my head, he put something in my lap, moved my hand until it touched the side. Waxed cup, extra large.

"The lid's off. Whatever you do, don't aspirate your vomit. I can't stop the plane to give you CPR."

Nice guy, who would go mouth-to-mouth with someone needing a barf cup.

"I'm all right," I said and choked on the last word as it got mixed with my breakfast. Napkins found my hand. I spat, wiped my mouth, opened my watering eyes.

"Don't worry, it happens to everyone. I get airsick myself."

He handed me a lid that I snapped onto the cup an instant before the plane hit another pothole. He took the cup of used Cheerios and lodged it on the floor behind him, next to a strapped-down fire extinguisher.

"When my mom flies," he said, "she wants us doing loops and rolls. She's the only one in the family with an astronaut's stomach. My sister won't get in the plane with her."

"Good for your sister." He didn't say anything so I asked, "Where do they live?"

"North of Orlando. Little town where Mom's fire chief." He looked past me at a sky gray and dense with clouds. We were coming down where the air was smoother. The water didn't look inviting, a field of frozen dark lava.

"There was a storm south of here yesterday. That's why it's still a little rough. What you're looking for is down there, at two o'clock."

A clump of mangrove sprawled on the Gulf of Mexico, so dense its greens were muddy black. As we drew closer, he tilted down the passenger wing just as the trees erupted with thousands of birds disturbed by the engine noise. They were as dense as cumulus clouds until they rose higher and dispersed, then they became a bright winter blizzard. I recognized frigate birds and herons, but there were many I couldn't identify.

We had been in the air for almost an hour, circling a dozen small keys and mangrove islands.

"It looks okay," I said. "Does it have a name?"

He looked at the chart spread on his knees. "If that was Snake Key behind us, this is Frigate Key, and it's a state nature preserve. There's really nowhere to go ashore. If you did, there's nothing to walk on but guano."

He circled lower, driving a few stalwart egrets from the trees.

"You really don't want to go ashore," he said.

"But a person could, in theory."

"A person could do a lot of dumb things."

"Thanks."

"The nature clubs come out to count eggs. The rules say they can't take a boat into the mangrove. So they wade ashore from about a hundred yards. At low tide it's never deeper than your waist. Maybe on you it would be a little deeper. Cold this time of year, too."

As the wing dipped, he said, "Take a look over on the east side."

It took me a moment to get my bearings of east and west. A small beach, which could have been made of sand or bird shit, met the shoaling water.

"Let's land," I said.

"You're the customer."

Inside the reef, the chop wasn't bad. We came down smoothly off the island's east side and drifted until we were about fifty yards from shore. The engine chortled at low rpms as he used the rudder to hold position. From here the mangrove stretched like open arms threatening an embrace. Pushing open the door, I looked at the water lapping the floats. This was the pink conch-decorated plane with a clubfoot. We didn't seem to be sinking.

"So?" he said.

"Now I need to use your radio."

He switched VHF bands, and I raised the marine operator, asked for a link to the Key West Police Department. The woman who answered said Sergeant Irvington was off-duty for the weekend. I left a message for him: *I found what I was looking for.* I went through the same routine with the Miami ATF office before turning the handset over to Steve.

"Are you lying to the police?" he said.

He really was an innocent.

"No. We expected bird shit and found it."

"Good you let them know."

He looked through the wind screen. For the past few minutes the birds had been wheeling back and settling like an explosion in reverse. We were drifting toward the shallows. Turning the rudder, he nudged us away from the shore. He took off his sunglasses and hung them on a shirt pocket.

"So what are you trying to do?" he asked. "Mess with some cops' heads?"

"That's always worth doing."

"You don't want to tell me?"

"No."

"Is what you're doing dangerous?"

"Compared to flying with you?" He grunted, and I proved I remembered. "You're the bold pilot, Luis is the old pilot."

"Luis lives for the chance to bomb Havana. Bottles of gasoline from two hundred feet."

"Is he serious?"

"He thinks so." Steve touched the rudder control. "I guess he is. There's a photograph of Jose Marti on his living room wall."

My mind was elsewhere. I asked, "Who is Jose Marti?" then mentally kicked myself for sounding like an idiot. But he got to tell me what I already knew.

"Cuban revolutionary of the old school. Patron saint of all factions."

Out near the north end of the island, tree branches shook as a few thousand birds rearranged themselves.

"I think we can head back now," I said.

Coming in, we would be visible to the entire town. Avila had eyes and ears. I wanted to be noticed. *You see that Cessna with pink conch shells on the side, that's the one she is on.*

And he would come looking for me.

26

Barry Irvington must have planned as he drank his way through Friday night to have Saturday morning for undisturbed recovery, perhaps fortified by a couple more of the same. I had spoiled the Saturday morning part of the plan. We were sitting at a diner in the new part of the island, the part built on fill, where nobody tried for quaint or picturesque. The biggest commercial tenant was Sears. The motels packed college students eight to a room. He had chewed me out when he found me at Bennell's office, and he remained angry.

He had made several points more than once.

First, there were no leaks in the Key West Police Department, so what was the purpose of my stunt?

Second, Nash and White were even more easily

insulted than a Key West policeman.

Third, if Avila somehow got the message, he would kill me.

"When he asks what you know, he'll have a knife at your throat. What *do* you know?"

"Nothing."

He rubbed his face, fished around in a voluminous suit pocket and brought out a bottle of buffered aspirin. "Give me a sip of your soda. Apart from waiting for Avila to come after you, do you have anything planned for today?"

"No."

"Then you can tag along with me."

Filled with sunlight, the Yates house felt only a little neglected, as if the family was gone for a long weekend. Nothing worse. A real estate agent would ask the customer to look past the housekeeping lapses to appreciate the imaginative layout, the clever use of light, the generous flow of space. *The estate is asking a million eight.*

In the daylight, the money that had been spent on decorating was more apparent. Glazed tiles brightened the floor. Bold primitive paintings hung in the main rooms. I wasn't sure how good they were but they hadn't been turned out by the local art factories. Keys pastel paintings are easy on tourists' eyes, and these were harsh and jarring. Small pieces of sculpture occupied niches high in the dining room wall.

"Any thoughts?" Barry asked.

"Who searched the place?"

"We did. White and Nash had a go."

"Nobody found anything that matters?"

"No. When you were here with Avila, did you notice anything?"

"I didn't even notice the art. Is the stuff valuable?"

"So-so. Mrs. Yates was close to a lot of gallery people." He walked a few steps, pointed to a shelf holding three carved stone heads that looked Central American. The faces were flat and brutish. "Here is where Aztec Rarities comes in. Maybe how Avila and Voss met the Yates family. These pieces are decent copies, according to a local dealer, not the kind meant to fool anyone. Importers bring them in by the container load."

"Aztec Rarities imported them?"

"Enough to keep a small shop stocked. But Avila and Voss weren't pottery dealers. And they weren't drug dealers. Nobody smuggles dope this way anymore. The only federal people interested in them have been the ATF team."

"And Mayor Yates was involved?"

"Probably."

"It doesn't look like he was hurting."

"Whatever mortgages could buy. If he came into money, it explains why he never looked back."

He locked the house and we walked to his car. On a low limestone wall, a snowy egret eyed us with disdain for predators who couldn't fly.

27

Both of Hub Bennell's boats at Sailhook were buttoned up tight, with no sign of the embittered captain or his unpaid crew. Barry stood on the pier watching a party aboard a cigarette boat that was tied at a neighboring slip. The group's three women boaters wore small bikinis.

"When I get my pension," he said, "I still won't be able to afford one of those."

"A blonde or the brunette?"

"Either. It would be a shallow life anyway."

"You didn't really think Avila would come back here?" I said.

"I thought we would look."

The office had no record of a boat called *Morning Glory*. The only vintage Chris Craft in the marina sat up front crowded with a Midwestern family. We walked through the place anyway. He could have switched boats, I thought. There were thirty or forty mid-sized, anonymous motor yachts that could have been worth closer inspection if we wanted to make the job impossible.

We went back and I climbed down into the rear cockpit of *Flyboy*. All the expensive fishing gear was out of sight. It could have been in the tall rod boxes that were padlocked on either side of the entrance to the salon, or the captain could have followed through on his threat to strip the boat. Fiberglass drapery hid the salon, and the sliding door to the interior was locked. I went forward around the cabin. Here the large windows were uncovered but I couldn't see very far into the living space. Without admitting it to my-self, I was looking for my client.

A Lexan hatch was set into the foredeck. You see what you expect to see.

For a moment, peering down into the tiny front ca-bin, I thought I had found Bennell. There was a man on the bunk directly below me. He lay naked and dis-figured, hands tied above his head, jaw sagging to one side with a spur of bone showing below the cheek, nose spread in a red pulp, blood around the hairline. He bore no resemblance to Hub except he was heavy-set. It took me several seconds to place where I had seen him.

"What are you doing on that boat?"

A woman in a Sailhook shirt was pointing her radio

at me and holding a clipboard aloft like a camp counselor. She took a heavy step from the pier to the
cockpit. I looked for Barry. He was standing at the
transom of the *Keys Pilot,* thirty feet away.

"There's a man—" I began. I got that much out.

The shock wave knocked me flat. I held my arms
over my head as the blast of hot air swept the deck.
Below me, fire boiled through the doorway beside the
man's bunk and the bedclothes burst into flame. The
heat in the cabin radiated through the Lexan. The
man's body hair ignited. His shoulders and legs con-
vulsed. The broken jaw widened as he screamed.
He locked eyes with me, full of awareness that there
was nothing to be done.

The plastic split and the hatch vented a geyser of
heat.

As I rolled away, fragments of wood and fiberglass
rained down. The woman in the Sailhook shirt was
scrambling onto the pier. That way was blocked for
me.

The boat was a crematorium.

28

Dusky room, pretty stencils near the ceiling.

A uniformed cop appeared in the doorway, stared a moment and vanished. I drifted off. A fat blond woman bent over me with a stethoscope. She amused herself and went away.

Barry Irvington was reading a magazine in the chair in the corner, sitting under a strong light, legs crossed, head bent. He looked battered, a bandage wrapping one hand, a ragged trouser leg exposing a pale shin. A brown sock, tasseled moccasin stained dark brown. He turned a page and noticed me watching.

"There was a man in the forward cabin," I said. I knew I had said it before. "On fire. Jim Riggs."

"He'd been bailed."

The back of my right hand, coated with spray-on bandage, was beginning to hurt. The side of my face felt greasy and numb.

"How badly am I burned?"

"First degree here and there. You're okay."

I settled back against the bed. "Where is this?"

"Islands Medical Center in Marathon. Do you re-member what happened? The boat was booby trapped. One of you set it off."

"Is the woman okay?"

Nodding, he tossed his magazine onto the bed. It was an issue of *Boating*.

"I called to you a couple of times to jump," he said. "I didn't think you were going to do it."

I didn't remember anyone's voice after the boom and was grateful I hadn't been able to hear the man in the cabin. The recollection of being in the water was faint. I knew Barry had pulled me out.

"Thanks," I said.

He acted as though I hadn't spoken. "I'm posting a guard here tonight," he said. "Terrence will be outside your room. Remember—big fists, thick head?"

"I want to leave."

"When the painkiller wears off, you'll be happy you're here."

I relented. Pump me full, keep me smiling, I thought.

"Riggs had been beaten. Tortured," I mumbled.

"You said so in the ambulance. Be glad it wasn't you." He looked at me with an expression I couldn't read, or didn't want to.

Nobody expects you to sleep in a hospital. Sleep might speed a recovery, leave an empty bed. A doctor came in around nine, bent on making sure I could grunt affirmatives while he talked. "You power boat people play hell with the reef," he said as he inspected a bandage I hadn't known I had. Left leg, puncture wound above the knee. He complimented himself on removing the plywood splinter and sewing neatly. "Your scar won't even be interesting. Do you know what motor oil does to living coral?"

"No."

"Kills it."

"So does fresh water," I said automatically.

"You don't feel guilty but you are. The longer-term effects on the ecosystem will be profound. We can't continue turning a blind eye to the damage you boat people do."

"I own a sailboat," I said.

He looked at me with practiced disappointment. Clearly I was avoiding coming to terms with my guilt.

"Sailboats pollute, too," he said.

A nurse woke me an hour and a half later disconnecting an IV. She left the door to the hallway open a crack, and I drifted off feeling grateful that someone was keeping the lights on to watch over me. Even if it was a blockhead like Officer Terrence.

29

*S*creaming.

The sound filled the hall, rattling to a crescendo. Then it sank to broken sobs. The screamer was a woman. She got going again before I was fully awake.

Getting out of bed in a modern hospital is no simple thing. Monitor leads stuck here and there took me time to undo, each yank evoking protests from the machine behind the bed. When I shuffled to the doorway, I was muzzy from sleep and drugs. The section of hallway that I could see was empty except for a wheelchair and an IV tree. Sobs came from somewhere beyond the T intersection down the hall.

I wobbled back and sat on the bed, not wanting to know about someone's nighttime tragedy. The burn on my hand felt new and alive. My thigh was stiff and painful. I had a few leftover aches and pains from before the boat blew up. As the painkiller wore off, so did my mental fuzz. I wondered whether Officer Terrence had gone to gawk at the screamer.

The room's metal wardrobe held my wet clothes bundled in a trash bag on the floor. Jeans, sweatshirt, underwear, sneakers. The hospital hadn't taken a position on whether the mess should be humanely destroyed. For all they knew it was everything I owned. I pulled off the hospital gown. As soon as I tugged on wet jeans I began shivering.

My gun was nowhere to be found. A bedside drawer held other personal items, nearly empty wallet, keys, watch, telephone, all resting on a towel.

I went down to the empty nurses station. The sobbing grew much closer.

Terrence was sitting on a bench twenty feet around the corner, comforting a woman whose face was hidden in her hands. Her weeping covered the sound of my approach. His eyes were fixed on a set of recessed double doors that led to the emergency room. When I looked through a window, activity in the room was coming to a standstill around a surgical table. My night nurse was removing an oxygen mask from a naked brown man on whom my doctor had turned his back. Three county policemen were at the head of the table, as immobile as the dead man.

I backed away from the door.

"Lonnie stopped a freak down on 940," Terrence

said. "The guy had a knife. How's he doing?"

The woman's head came up at the question.

"The doctor's in there," I said.

"*My Lonnie.*" Her face went into Terrence's big chest, muffling her howl.

"Was it Avila?" I said.

Terrence shook his head. "Probably not. You've got No Name Key up there. A lot of lowlifes. This guy's on foot. Even after getting cut, Lonnie shot up his car." He injected a note of admiration for the woman's benefit.

"Give me a ride out there," I said.

"Sergeant Irv said keep an eye on you."

"You can do that at the crime scene."

"I kinda got my hands full right now."

The grieving woman made a smothered protest and pushed away, then kept pushing empty space, telling him to go. He was squeezing her hands when two county cops came out of the emergency room and told her what a ballsy guy Lonnie had been.

30

If you drive Highway 940 on Big Pine Key on a hot summer night with the windows open, the mosquitoes will suck you dry to the music of alligators warbling. This damp January night was silent. Down the road a flashing light bar hung ahead of us, splashing the pines red. Terrence parked on the shoulder and got out.

A sporty red convertible was nearby, bathed in both sets of police lights. It appeared to have slid backward into roadside brush. A county cop was shining his flashlight onto the car's seats.

"I keep hoping I'll see blood. Be nice if Lonnie got him but he wasn't much of a shot."

"Looks like he got some tires."

"Would have been aiming at the perp's head."

Terrence stood with his thumbs in his belt. "I had his girlfriend crying on me. How do you tell her he was dumb and let the guy get too close?"

"His girlfriend or the wife?"

"I don't know. But do you tell her?"

"I don't think you do." The flashlight turned my way. "Who's this?"

"She's had a good look at Hector Avila."

His head snapped around.

"*Shee-it!*"

Two cruisers blew past us, accelerating toward the Overseas Highway. We hadn't heard a radio call.

"What are they doing?" I said.

"Hoping something falls into the headlights."

I pointed at a wall of trees that began twenty feet off the roadside. "What's back there?"

"A big pond on state property," the county cop said. "Past that pond are some streets, a dozen houses. That was the first area we searched. We had ten cars down there an hour ago. "

"She thinks we're chasing Avila."

"Could be. This car got boosted yesterday p.m. in Marathon. Where was your suspect then?"

It was close to three a.m. Sunday. I was losing track of time. Where had Avila been Saturday after-noon? I told them didn't know.

"We got no description of the car thief or Lonnie's killer. Avila's vitals are on the air. Five ten, a hundred fifty pounds, olive complexion, black hair. That sound right?"

"That sounds like everyone named Gomez," Terrence said.

The county officer walked to his cruiser. The radio band was full of reports all of a sudden. The reports were of nothing seen on Little Torch or the boat yard.

"Say it was your guy. Where would he go?"

"Are there any marinas down this road?" I said. "Any anchorages?"

"Plenty of private docks, but it's pretty shallow back there."

"Could a Chris Craft find a mooring?"

"How big?"

"Fifty-some feet."

"You wouldn't want to do it at night, but I expect so. Worst that would happen is you would run aground till high tide."

I went back to Terrence's car and sat with hot air blowing on me. Every time I looked at the trees I got worried. Avila was good in the dark. He would be good coming up behind the two cops. Then I got more worried. Any police cruiser shooting trough the dark miles of Highway 940 could have Hector Avila at the wheel. You wouldn't know it unless he stopped.

At five o'clock Terrence drove me back to the hospital. I settled the bill with a credit card and got my gun from their safe. The doctor wasn't in sight and nobody complained that I hadn't gotten a medical release.

Terrence took me home, came aboard with his H&K poking at shadows. After he went ashore, I locked the hatch and headed for my bunk. If there was a bomb under the mattress I would never know. I collapsed onto the stale sheets. Instead of finding the release of sleep I found myself thinking about how well Avila had evaded the nets thrown by local and federal cops.

I slept with my gun under the pillow.

31

At eight-thirty Sunday evening the Carbuncle was showing a pornographic video on the big screen above the bar, and Lemuel Rees was jeering the performances while challenging two scabrous bikers to match the players' agility. I drank diet ginger ale out of a can while adding up my day, which totaled nothing. I had slept through half of it, until pain in four distinct body parts woke me. Then I had knocked myself out with Roxicet until a little after six o'clock when Arthur Hawkes's mother let me use the office microwave at low heat to try to dry my phone. When I reinstalled the battery, the thing lit up and I called Barry, who said there was no sign of the *Morning Glory*.

Two helicopters had buzzed mangrove clumps and private docks over a hundred square miles of water behind No Name Key. Coast Guard patrols were stopping more than the usual number of pleasure boaters. Road blocks had been established along the Overseas Highway at Marathon and Key Largo. There were a lot of pissed-off boaters and drivers in the Keys. Otherwise, nada.

"He's probably back in Miami," Barry said.

I thought he underrated Avila's arrogance, but I hoped he was right.

Lem came down the bar and blew smoke in front of me. He shook my soda can, set it down. The place was crowded and noisy and he had to shout.

"There's talk going round that a guy could score some good rock off you," he said.

Talk going round. Too many people had time on their hands.

"Whose talk?"

"Hey, I'm no gossip." But he raised his scraggly eyebrows, which was as good as saying he liked the story and would repeat it.

"You could get me arrested," I said.

Indifferent shrug. So much for appealing to his decent side.

"Lemuel," I said breathily, as if I could barely keep my tongue from burrowing into his ear, "I could probably arrange to have cops crawling all over this dump on Saturday nights."

If you couldn't score crack at the Carbuncle on weekends, you couldn't get it anywhere. Which was like saying you couldn't get flat beer.

"You're balling the cop, huh?"

I let it pass. Better if Lem thought so. He put his elbows on the bar and ducked his face like a turtle's. "Thing is, there ain't no rumors about my regulars. People who might need a little something keep their mouths shut. The talk is about you."

"Whose talk?"

"A guy says you took over your pop's business."

Then I knew. "Let me guess, Lem. You've been listening to a big white boy in an ATF shirt."

As he coughed, the odor of his breath hit me. It was worse than the bar's perpetual chili. Wiping his lips, he said, "It wasn't that asshole." He held up a narrow hand with a little finger that bent outward at the second knuckle. "Nash broke this a year ago. I don't talk to him if I can help it."

"Who then?"

"Cuban guy. He came in this afternoon pretending he was mucho hombre. Dressed like a pimp."

I felt sick.

"Claimed he'd bought off you, off your old man before that. Got blowed by you for good measure. Don't get radical, I'm just telling you."

"It's okay, Lem. What else?"

"He asked when you came in. I said you don't punch a clock. Good one, huh?"

"Thank you."

"Sure, glad to help."

"If he shows up again, I want you to call a number for me. It's Sergeant Irvington. I know that goes against your religion, but he would be grateful."

"And so would you?" Eyes slitting, he grinned.

"That's right. I won't burn this dump down."

His grin widened. "You know, Meggie, you really look like shit."

He gave me a scrap of paper on which I wrote Barry's number. When Lem went off, I swiveled and looked at the crowd. Tonight he had everything from college students out for a roll in the dirt to aging locals who dodged the landlady so they could buy shots. People were standing, stomping, throwing darts, vanquishing bottles, even dancing cheek to cheek. There were parts of the room I couldn't see. Tables in corners. Single chairs hidden by posts or bodies. A few people close to me obscured whoever stood behind them.

I didn't think Avila was here, but I had too much painkiller in my system to trust my judgment.

The side door was the nearest way out. I got off the stool. A glimpse of a shape behind a post, vaguely male, froze me. But he was Anglo and blond. A dazed girl staggered across my path trying out as a poster chick for roofers. Heavy shoulders in a rugby shirt blocked the view to my right. An opening came and I shortened the distance to the door by several feet, saw Avila near the pool table until his face refocused as neighboring boat owner. There was a blow at my back and I gasped in panic, knowing it was a knife. A sweaty pink face came around and said, "You wanna drink?"

I pushed the door open and went out and planted my back against the wall. I hoped no one came out after me because the .380 was in my palm and I didn't want to shoot anyone while a little stoned.

The Carbuncle's back parking lot got a trace of light from the sky. Artificial lighting would have reduced the privacy inside the cars. My free hand glided off fenders and doors as I worked around to the side of the building. A couple of junk trees tilted against the eaves like rooted customers. A dark Miata came in from the road and nosed around for a parking slot.

I got to the front, where red neon filled the windows. I started across the road.

A figure stood under the street lamp outside the marina. He stood hipshot, arms folded, belly hanging over the waistband of his shorts, legs as skinny and white as a chicken's. Arthur Hawkes looked across the road hungrily. His mother had banned her middle-aged son from the Carbuncle, where he spent too much money on Bahama Village girls. He turned and trudged back into the marina.

Avila was ten feet to my left.

"*Tenia negocios con su padre.*"

My Spanish was good enough for that.

"I used to do business with your father."

He stepped out of the shadows, hands empty. I raised the gun and aimed at the pale blur of his chest.

"In Santiago de Cuba—"

"Shut up," I said.

I risked a glance to the right. If you're right-hand

dominant, in theory it's the easiest way to look without disturbing an aim, the easiest to look back from. There was no sign of Pinky or Che. I stole a glance toward the marina. All I could say for certain was that the road was empty for thirty feet in both directions. Behind me might be a different story.

"Put your hands out from your sides," I said.

He did as he was told. My phone was wedged in a front pocket. As I pulled it out, his chin went up. I pulled up the antenna with my teeth.

"Your father would listen," he said.

"Don't move."

"This will be difficult for you to accept, but Daniel worked with me for two years before his death." His voice was calm, the soft push of a salesman who knew his product was irresistible. "He wanted to be-lieve he was an idealist. That meant he could not work any longer against oppressed people, not for so little money as the CIA offered."

I didn't miss the mockery—*for so little money* was the point.

"You're a liar," I said. My phone display was dark. Not enough baking. My mind wasn't fully dried out either. But I tried. I backed toward the front door of the tavern.

"Where did you find my boat?"

So it was the boat.

"I didn't find a damn thing," I said. "It was a ruse."

"My boat, its cargo, my money—they are all miss-ing." He had put on a frown of brooding sensuality.

"I'm not the brute you think."

"I'll ask Mrs. Yates."

"They cheated me, she and her husband."

There was a burst of noise behind me as the bar's door opened and footsteps crunched on gravel. A car door clicked open but didn't close. A man spoke in a half-drunk Florida drawl.

"Look at that honey with the gun. Go tell Lem."

"Call the police!" I shouted over my shoulder.

"Perhaps I should have let Che kill you," Avila said.

"What did you do to Hub?"

There were footsteps behind me. I smelled booze, and big arms reached around me. "Hey, honey, you shouldn't be pointing that thing." He grabbed for my wrist, and I pushed out of his grasp. As I spun away, I saw Avila moving.

"Stop, goddammit!"

The big guy bumped my arm as I fired. He grabbed again for my wrist. I kicked out, didn't really connect, but he let go and I ran onto the road. Avila was a hundred yards from the tavern. At the next intersection, a police cruiser turned onto the road. There hadn't been time for a call from the Carbuncle, so this was part of the patrol covering the island. When the headlights illuminated Avila, he staggered to the roadside and sank to his knees. He was clutching his abdomen. I knew my shot hadn't struck him.

The light bar came on as the car stopped and a woman got out. I wondered if it had happened like this up in Big Pine, the injured little immigrant begging for help. She was too far away to make sense of my warning. She extended a hand, and Avila pulled her down and stabbed. She went to her knees.

He had reversed the car and driven into Bahama Village before I reached the policewoman. Her shoulders twitched. Her eyes reproached the group closing in on her. She tried to reach one-handed for the knife that wobbled between her shoulder blades. Then she settled onto her elbows with her teeth gritted.

"What'd he do?" she said.

"He stabbed you."

"Afraid of that." She had a narrow, lined face. "Hurts like shit."

"That's good," I said. I didn't know. "Tell me how to use your radio."

I notified the dispatcher they had an officer down near the Carbuncle and gave a description of Avila. Two Conchs were kneeling beside the cop, telling her they thought she was doing okay. They knew better than to touch the knife.

People were trickling out of the bar. Lem Rees was nowhere to be seen.

I could still see the stolen cruiser's light strobing somewhere down in Bahama Village, and I headed after it.

32

The police car straddled the intersection two blocks into the narrow streets. The doors and windows of the tiny houses bled television noise and music. A man with a bottle stood in a doorway, having forgotten that people in Bahama Village don't always benefit from face-to-faces with the local law.

Charging along with a gun in my hand, I was asking to get shot by the first cop who spotted me. But the sirens were a couple of blocks back.

I'd had my chance, listening to the cold bastard when I should have shot him. That was all it took, someone saying *Let me tell you about your daddy* froze my brain. I wanted to hear.

There was no sign of Avila beyond the empty car. Noticing my dilemma, the man in the doorway turned his head left. I could believe him or not. If he steered me wrong, he wouldn't be as likely to get to see a shooting. I went left.

At the next corner, a lace-curtain restaurant was serving ethnic food at tourist prices. I opened the front door and looked inside. A half-dozen faces were indifferent to everything except soft jazz and chittlins.

I backed out and put away my gun.

Ramshackle houses lay in every direction. Dogs were barking. Roosters crowed. Crossing the street, I glanced into yards where a little light reached among the washing machines and chicken wire. If he had found cover he would have night vision by now. I moved past another house. In the back yard a chain clinked as an animal paced.

Red light flashed across the house fronts. I walked out into the street, hands empty, in front of a slow-moving police cruiser. The driver, whom I knew by sight, shined his spotlight where I directed between houses. All we saw were the maniacal eyes of a Rottweiler.

With a shotgun on his shoulder, the cop walked as far as the dog's territory.

An old man leaned from a side doorway. "Somebody was back there. Ambrose don't talk unless someone's bothering him." He nodded. "The reverse is true too. Whoever you're after is long gone or Ambrose would still be having his say."

We walked to the end of the block.

"He's going to get away again," I said.

The cop shook his head. "Not tonight. He's got his back to the water. In five minutes we'll have this whole end of the island sealed off." He was swinging the flashlight back and forth, shining it into side yards. "The boys at the Carbuncle said you tried to make a citizen's arrest. That right?"

"Yeah."

I thought he was going to tell me how I had screwed up.

"Pretty gutsy. Come on. I'll give you a ride to the command post."

In the middle of Whitehead Street, police cars sat at hundred-foot intervals. The center of activity was a six-wheeled van with no markings on the doors. Men in dark suits were walking in circles talking into chin microphones. Uniformed locals stood aside. Yellow tape strung along the lamp poles held back a crowd lured from bars and motels. A few people were ducking back and forth under the tape, carrying big drink cups. They knew that whatever happened in Key West would be a party.

Randy Nash came up alongside me. He wore a dark jacket and a baseball cap and had a machine gun tucked under his arm. "I'm keeping an eye on you," he said.

I walked away from him.

Uniformed men and a couple of women piled into cars and sped into the dilapidated neighborhood. "Emma Street," someone said. I slipped across the street and followed the cars on foot. The cross street

was a claustrophobic lane between frame houses
built right against the sidewalks. The houses had
been slave houses before Secession. I didn't know
what to call them now. A few kids had come outdoors, acting brazen while there was no one to take
them up on it.

Close behind I heard steps. I started to turn when
a hand pushed my shoulder and I flew into a board
wall. The impact knocked me down.

"Told you I was gonna keep an eye on you."

Face red, Nash closed in as I pushed myself off the
street. He said, "Come on, get up so I can pretend
I'm a sporting man."

My left shoulder was numb to the elbow. My
cracked rib was on fire. I felt tears running down my
face and told myself they came from anger.

"I'm going to get your friend Avila."

I held my teeth tight. "You'll beat the shit out of him
if he's a woman. Otherwise," I said, "he'll have your
fucking pants around your ankles."

He stared at me and caught a glimpse of what I
saw hiding beneath the macho strut, butch hair, bristled chin. Randy Nash's proper habitat was a nursing
home where all the patients were weak and accus-
tomed to keeping silent. I sat on the cracked pavement, wary of his feet, because he looked ready to
kick me. "I don't work for Avila," I said. "My father
didn't. You can believe what you like."

He was breathing heavily, clenching and unclench-
ing his right hand as he sized up the street for wit-

nesses. He said something I could barely hear.

"Your old man got in the way of a good operation."

"Did he know he was in the way?"

"He didn't care. We would have shut Avila down, maybe wrapped up some of his friends. Instead we looked like jerks."

He backed off a reasonable distance while I got up.

"If you want to look for the bastard, stay with me. You're better off if you've got company."

I forced myself not to laugh. In less than a minute he had gone from being my attacker to my protector.

"You gonna mention this?" he asked.

If I could find a witness, I might make an assault complaint stick in about a thousand years.

"No, I'm not going to," I said.

"Why not?"

Because you're nuts, I thought, and dangerous.

"Let's skip it," I said. "Tell me about Avila's boat. What was it carrying?"

"Guns, explosives, money. He's a freelance trafficker. The Cuban government trusts him."

He was half a step ahead of me when we reached the corner. Radios were audible a block away, where a half-dozen official cars had converged at a three-story wooden building. A blond cop passed us going the opposite direction. A radio in his fist was spitting orders. At the sound of gunfire, Nash broke into a trot.

A sign above the building's front stairway identified the Gibbons Brothers Mortuary. Most of the windows were boarded. Half of a third-floor balcony had collapsed onto a porch roof. Light flickered inside the building, visible in the cracks between window boards.

"Neighbor called he'd seen someone go in there," a local cop told Nash.

"Who's shooting?"

The policeman laughed. "A county boy killed a shadow."

"Who's inside?"

"Sergeant Irvington and two other guys."

Four men in vests rushed the porch, and the radio noise intensified. In front of us, men leaned on fenders aiming long guns at the building in case it tried to run. I worried about Barry getting hit by friendly fire.

"They always climb," someone said.

"Not always. I had one that hid in a furnace."

"They usually climb."

Two shots banged on an upper floor, and a voice near me said, "See."

They brought him out after ten minutes. The creamy shirt was blood-soaked, and there was a bandage around his upper arm. Barry came behind, pulling off a vest.

The prisoner turned his head, and I got a good look. He had dark skin. His round face was wide-eyed and open-mouthed and fearful. I had never seen him before.

Avila was still out there.

33

I woke in total darkness.

It was disconcerting not to remember where I was, where I had been anytime recently, whether my mother was right about the paint color for her house at the lake, whether I could find someone I was looking for. Whether I had a chance of passing final exams. Instead of studying I had been horsing around somewhere I didn't belong. The dream worries fell away one by one. When I realized I didn't face final exams, I burrowed into the pillow in relief. The house had been painted three summers ago. Mom was happy with our jointly chosen color scheme. But who had I been looking for? Then I was awake enough to remember that Dad wasn't hiding on some godforsaken key, he had drowned. Of course. That was it.

I kept my face buried in the pillow. It was Barry's pillow, his daybed. I squinted at my watch, wondering why I was awake. Three hours since my head had hit the pillow. There had been a muffled thump as I swam up out of the dream. The sound had been like the contact of a sailboat with its bumpers, and for a few seconds I had dreamed I was aboard the *Key-Hole*. Lifting my head, I saw a crack of light under the kitchen door. Another soft thud, this time the door to the refrigerator. I didn't get up. I didn't want to talk to Barry any more tonight. He had offered me a safe crib, out of Avila's reach, and I had accepted. He was a gentleman. We hadn't discussed where I would sleep, or whether he was too old for me—mid-fifties, I guessed, and maybe that wasn't too old—or too homely, or too close to bald. The subject hadn't come up. The apartment barely registered on me. Shooting trophies in the living room, dirty socks on the kitchen table, no wonder Mrs. Irvington had run off.

I got up, washed my face and headed back to the daybed.

Barry was in the kitchen doorway. I had never made it a priority to learn what middle-aged bachelors wear to bed. Barry had on ancient sweat pants, a Conch Republic T-shirt and battered topsiders.

"Come on," he said, "let's do some sensible talking."

I sat at the kitchen table. He popped a can of Coke and poured it into two small square glasses.

"I've been on the phone to Agent White at ATF.

The guy we caught was a nobody. He said a rich man had been paying him fifty a day for access to his uncle's mortuary. If Terrence could shoot better, that deal would have cost the guy his life."

"Avila needed a base here."

"The man thinks the person he dealt with was a policeman. He was there putting on his uniform tonight. He had been undercover earlier. Gave his landlord his expensive shirt. The only thing that jarred was he also put on a blond wig tonight."

It took me a moment. Then I pictured the blond policeman who had been running away from the action.

"He ran right past Nash and me."

"He went past a half-dozen uniformed officers." Barry leaned back. "Avila should be shot for making us look bad. Your buddy Randy Nash, in fact, plans to shoot on sight."

"My buddy knocked me on my ass when no one was looking."

"I'll talk to him."

"No. He decided we'll be pals. That's enough for now."

He stood up, looked at the clock. "This morning we're going to try some salvage work. We know where to begin looking for *Two Earls*, don't we?"

"Keys with dense mangrove."

"It's been five months. Someone would have found it. My bet it's on the bottom."

"Then we're out of luck, aren't we?"

"We know where you father's boat was found. I

think we should start there and work backward. Do you want breakfast?"

He scrambled eggs and made toast as I showered. There was still no sign of daylight as we ate.

"Yates could have gotten away with the boat and its cargo," I said.

"If he'd made it to any port, the guns would have come on the market. Avila would have found out. He believes whatever was on board is still out there. So does ATF."

"I guess there could be a promotion for whoever gets there first," I said.

"Could be. But there's something even better. If we find the boat, ATF will get a chance to kiss my ass. And yours."

"I'll settle for a handshake," I said.

34

The owner of the boat that Barry had lined up was named Ellsworth Hobbes. He was at least six-foot-three and wore a close-cropped goatee that elongated his face and made him look taller. Short white hair formed a dagger-like widow's peak at the front. His thick black neck was decorated with a string of tiny lavender shells. He wore a collarless striped shirt, white duck shorts, sandals over bare feet. He had swung me on board one-handed while clapping Barry on the shoulder in welcome.

Hobbes had worked narcotics with Metro-Dade before taking disability retirement on a hip wound and buying a drug mule's boat at auction. The boat's big canopied deck was perfect for hauling large groups on boozy diving trips to the Marquesas. Hobbes kidded the tourists that he was running *ganja* in the hold beneath their feet.

"Doing it right now," he said, deciding I was almost a tourist. We were motoring out of the Garrison Bight.

"Good line of work for an ex-cop," I said.

"Dope is like penicillin. Cures what ails you."

"Ellsworth isn't the best dive captain on the island," Barry said, "but he's the only one who works for nothing."

"I had to cancel four paying customers this morning," the captain said.

The boat rode heavily, as if the hold might indeed be loaded with contraband. The engines hammered to create forward momentum but failed to prevent the occasional sea from taking us broadside, spraying over the low canvas railings. After trusting me with the wheel, Hobbes smoked an oversweet pipe and chatted with other captains on the radio.

We reached open water doing twelve knots ahead of a turbulent wake that a couple of seabirds trailed. The wind was strong. I wore a heavy sweater of Barry's. Hobbes tended his pipe, which sprinkled embers on the plank deck.

"I stayed on the boat last night," Hobbes said. "Felt I should have paid something for the show you folks put on. You didn't catch anyone, did you?"

"We shot an innocent bystander," Barry said. "That counts for something."

"How innocent?"

"Not completely."

"Points off. The show looked over-copped. I saw some ATF jackets, no FBIs."

"They couldn't find the address."

Hobbes grunted. "We know about the paper gun squad."

"Yeah, we do."

"Fucking Bad Investigators. You think Avila is still around?"

"Yes."

"Big ego?"

"Smarter than all of us put together. And tougher. If you see a Chris Craft, you may want to hide down below."

"Sure, I don't want to bring my shotgun upstairs where it'll get damp."

"What's in it?"

"Number four."

"Have you been having trouble out here?"

"Not a bit. That surprise you?"

"Not a bit," Barry said.

Forty minutes west of the town, Ellsworth Hobbes throttled down and took us below decks. In the cramped, musty-smelling space, wooden bins were loaded with snorkel masks, fins, weight belts, spongy zippered wetsuits. None of the gear hinted at prosperity. I could see small holes in the nearest wetsuit. Some of the masks were cloudy.

The head was a plywood cell back near the engine compartment. When I came out, Hobbes was busy at the bow, opening a padlocked compartment. He smiled proudly as he flipped toggle switches and elec-tronic screens lit up.

"Lady who owned her was making rendezvous with little rafts full of cocaine," he said. "The rafts had low-power transmitters with a range of less than a mile, so she had to know where she was. So I've got two-year-old Leica GPS charting, Wide Area Augmenta-tion, fish finder, and side-scan sonar. Perfect for what I wanted."

"What was that?" I said.

"Nothing to do with fish," he said.

I wondered if he was raiding drug-runners.

"Ellsworth likes to keep his hobby quiet," Barry said. "If you bring a load up from the bottom officially, Uncle Sam may fight you for it."

"A load of what?"

"Spanish treasure." Ellsworth Hobbes grinned, eyes lit with passion.

"At best you get to keep only some of what you re-cover," Barry said. "But if you bring it up on the q.t., you don't have to share."

"Yeah. But the main reason for security is I don't want my brains blown out by some fool for two doub-loons," Hobbes said. "If I ever hit the mother lode, there's no way to keep the recovery operation secret. I would have to syndicate it with one of the bigger groups. For snooping around, I dive single-handed or my son comes down from Miami."

Despite myself I was smiling. "Do you find much?"

"She thinks I'm nuts, Irv. You're asking the wrong

question, honey. I've got my pension, so I don't need to find a thing. Worst case, I get my exercise and have fun. The right question is whether there's anything down there left to find. You look back on the records, roughly half of whatever sank off Florida is still under us, probably a couple of billion worth. It's just a lot harder get to these days. All the easy wrecks have probably been found. The storms that took the ships down scattered the cargo and buried it. So you've got to be able to ping the bottom to detect metal. Then you need to move a lot of sand, and that's where syndication comes in."

"How long have you been looking?"

"Ten months, starting a week after I retired." One of the screens was lighted in three colors. Darker lines etched a smooth pattern that he identified as the Gulf's bottom.

"How deep?" Barry said.

"Right below us, thirty feet. A quarter mile north you could stand on the bottom when the tide's out. What kind of boat are we looking for?"

"Fifty-three-foot Hatteras without its flying bridge. The transom probably says *Two Earls*."

"How long has it been here?"

"Five months."

"I'm familiar with a lot of the junk that's been on the bottom a while. Even so, you got about a million square miles to cover, and we're going to hear a lot of false alarms."

"We can narrow it down some." Barry explained

about the drifting boat. Twenty-four hours at the outside for the period of drift. Most of the time with the sail empty of air, the boat riding the current. Say one knot, on average. That created a megaphone shaped search pattern, beginning where *KeyHole* was found and expanding as we moved west.

Hobbes made an immediate correction. "The drift would have been southeast. So we'll work northwest. Are you sure the boat sank?"

"We're guessing. Could be wrong."

"What's she carrying?"

"ATF thinks guns."

Hobbes sighed. "Is there anything you know for sure, Irv?"

"Not that I can think of."

"This is really promising." Hobbes put his hands on his hips. "Here's how we'll do it. You go up, Irv, and set the course I tell you. I'll sit and watch the bottom. I used to have a monitor topside, but two of them got stolen."

I said, "The screen shows you sunken treasure?"

"Mostly it shows me fish. There's a dual frequency echo sounder that pings the bottom, and a chip translates the echoes into a picture. Then I've got this bundled with software from a company called Garrett, which makes metal detectors." He pointed to the bottom right quadrant of the screen. "I added this. Problem is, the sea bottom's full of trash metal."

"What are the chances of finding the boat?" I said.

He rubbed his goatee. "You never know. The

echo sounder's got a range of a thousand feet, the Garrett a little less. We can ignore the small hits. On a modern fiberglass boat, most of the metal is in the engine. That's what we want. But anything with an iron keel that went down in the last fifty years will make a lot of noise. And we've probably got a few ocean-going barges down there. And steel-hulled lifeboats from the war. Who knows?"

We got underway, and he pulled two fishing rods from a rack. He offered me the rods, showed me a cooler that held a small pail of chopped fish.

"If you drop a line over the side, we may have lunch," he said. "Don't let the pelicans steal it."

I boated four snapper in forty-five minutes. Hobbes cooked them off the stern on a gas grille with sides of potatoes and onions. We sat drifting while we ate. We were miles beyond the reef that protected Key West and the Marquesas, and the swells rolled in hard and heavy.

35

At mid-afternoon Hobbes scrambled topside and pushed back the throttle. As the boat lost momentum, he turned the wheel so we began circling.

"Do we drop anchor?" Barry said.

"I'll take a look first. Try to hold our position." He went below and returned a minute later in a wetsuit with an air tank over his shoulder. He struggled with a pair of fins, then checked his regulator's air flow. In a few seconds he was over the side dropping from sight in the cloudy water. I wondered what we would do if he didn't reappear after a reasonable time. There seemed to be only one set of tanks on board.

He surfaced in three minutes.

"It's a plane," he reported. "An old Lance II, been down there a few months. Looks like he stripped everything out and was hauling marijuana." He clambered aboard, shedding gear and water. "I thought about explaining the basics of load, fuel and distance to the pilot, but he's got little fishes swimming out his eye sockets."

He looked up as the sound of an engine reached us. A little distance off the bow, a small high-winged plane turned toward our boat and dropped to a hundred feet above the water. As he zoomed overhead, the wings tipped back and forth and a hand waved from the cockpit. Stretching from under the canopy, Hobbes waved back.

"That's Puny Greer, taking the foolhardy to the Tortugas."

"He's five miles south of where he should be," Barry said.

"Puny flies by dead reckoning. He can't read a chart, doesn't trust compasses. When he gets farther out he'll climb till he spots the islands."

Hobbes ordered another stop an hour later. Then as the boat circled, he decided the signal wasn't strong enough to justify a dive.

By five o'clock he had strapped the tanks on twice more and inspected a drowned Volkswagen and the bow of a World War II submarine. Two more red X's on his treasure-hunting charts. He was pushing the limit on descents. He shivered as another plane brayed overhead. For the last hour we had been on the direct path of Tortugas traffic. The plane was high, its fuselage reflecting sunlight. I couldn't tell if the pilot was Puny Greer or Steve Taylor or someone else. Barry watched the aircraft shrink to a flickering spark in the distance.

It would be easy for Avila to find us out here. If he did, he wouldn't move in until he believed we had found something.

At five-thirty, Ellsworth Hobbes said he was through diving for the day. The air was cooler. The sky in the east was sooty blue, finally empty of planes but busy with cartwheeling pelicans and cormorants. Hobbes threw a beer can overboard to confuse the next searchers.

"It's time to head in," he said.

"We'll find a well-lighted place for dinner," Barry said.

"Sounds good, Irv. Sorry this was a bust."

While Barry turned the boat, Hobbes sat beside me. He looked big and dangerous. "I been wondering something since Irv introduced us. How do you know this Avila dude?"

"Friend of the family."

"What kind of family? You don't look like a gun-runner."

"Neither do you."

"Her father got her into the business," Barry said.

"Lay off," I said. "Just for a change, let's talk about your family."

"Ellsworth already knows that story. Jacob Irvington was a Philadelphia cop who ate every meal on the badge. He retired at sixty-two and lived another fifteen years in Vero Beach with Mom. They died two years apart."

"That's why Irv became a cop, so he could eat for free," Hobbes said.

"But I pay for my own drinks," Barry said.

"You'd break the saloons otherwise." Hobbes glanced at me, still curious, then got up and went below to shut down the electronics. In a minute he climbed back up, stripping off his sweatshirt.

"I think we found something," he said.

36

He broke surface a few feet from the boat and struggled to the ladder. I reached the canvas railing as Hobbes stretched out of the water and slid a long black cylinder onto the deck. It looked like a section of stove pipe closed at both ends.

"What's this?" Barry said.

"Goes boom," said Hobbes.

He climbed the ladder halfway, then rested his head on his arms.

"There's a fifty-some-foot Hatteras called *Two Earls* sitting on the bottom at forty feet," he said. "It hasn't been there forever and it didn't sink yesterday. Four dead folks on the inside bridge. Crates of these things and other goodies among the remains."

He flung a small mesh bag across the deck, then

came the rest of the way on board. As he sagged onto a bench shivering, I handed him a towel.

"You went inside?" Barry said.

"Not past the bridge. There was more stuff stacked beside the ladder to the salon."

"What sort of stuff?"

"RPGs--grenades you fire off the end of a rifle. Ten boxes." His breathing slowed. He touched a foot to the black tube. "And crates of these. You know what this is?"

"Either a drain pipe or a launcher."

"You small town cops are sad. There are at least thirty of them down there. Stinger type surface to air missiles. Last year I had druggies trying to buy Stingers to shoot down our surveillance dirigible Fat Albert. The printing on these crates looks Arabic."

"Are they operational?"

"The cylinder's supposed to be air tight. I wouldn't point it at my foot to find out."

"What's the condition of the bodies?"

"Scattered bones. I saw four skulls. One had an extra eye hole." He touched his forehead.

"Did you bring up anything to identify the bodies?"

"Like jaw bones?"

"Wallets or rings."

He pointed to the mesh bag. Barry spread a tarp on the deck, and they dumped the bag's contents. Hobbes had made a soggy collection of billfolds, credit cards, laminated driver's licenses, a plastic-jacketed passport. Barry lifted the passport. The cover still bore faint ornate lettering *Estados Unidos Mexicanos.* He opened the pages carefully. The name inside was Eduardo Laguna Soriano. The photograph retained only a muddy image of a mustached, square-faced man with widely spaced eyes.

"What else do we have?" He put the passport aside, picked up a lizard-skin folder. Hundred-dollar bills, credit cards and a driver's license spilled out. The license had been issued by the State of Florida to a nerdy looking man named Cole Robert Yates. Barry handed the license to Ellsworth Hobbes.

"What was he doing?"

"Hijacking his friend's guns, maybe."

Barry looked at me. Then he went back to sorting.

"Pemex card for Laguna Soriano. Florida driver's license for Julia Mercado. Who were these people? Amex card for Robert Ball, Visa for Ralph Berman, Visa for Robert Bates. Either they were having a convention out here, or someone had a few aliases." He paused, then handed me a laminated identification card issued by the United Nations. Through the fogged plastic I saw a narrow face, high cheeks, slightly protruding front teeth, receding dark hair. No one I recognized. The card identified Julian Torres as a Cuban delegate to the United Nations.

"Is that all the names?" I said.

"I may have missed something, and I didn't check the salon or the cabins," Hobbes said. "I can't go down again today. Decompression time is cumulative. What do you make of this, Irv?"

"Arms deal turned into a hijacking? Hijacking went sour? Have you got any thoughts, Meggie?"

"No."

He didn't look as though he believed me. Looked as if he'd considered, just for a second, how I'd insisted on staying in town for the last few months without a good reason.

"Did you find any money?" I asked. "Avila said his money disappeared, too."

"Just what you see."

The boat rode down a swell, and the sun was out of sight. It was evening under the canopy.

"Let's put off supper," Barry said. "Much as I hate to, I've got to talk to some people."

37

The satchel's contents spilled onto spread newspapers covering the desk in Barry's office. I wasn't as interested this time. Deputy Chief Pohl fed himself Chinese noodles as he watched the two ATF agents, White and Nash, who stared down at the pile of documents. Both men looked like someone had thrown a party and not invited them.

"Cuban diplomat, Mexican national—who are they?" Barry said.

Randy Nash pretended not to hear. "Where's the boat?"

Barry didn't answer.

Nash glared at Pohl, who continued to eat.

Ernie White spoke. "The Mexican guy who called himself Laguna Soriano was a buyer for the Mexican

Revolutionary Popular Army. *Ejercito Popular Revo-lucionario*. They're down in Chiapas province, vague-ly Marxoid, shooting at the federals and holding press conferences. The Mercado woman was probably part of that group, but I don't recognize the name. They were on a buying trip about six months ago, picking up heavier weapons. Torres would have been the supplier."

"His card says he was a UN diplomat."

"Ain't it nice? He's used Avila before as a go-between. Is the money on the boat?"

"Why a go-between?"

"Cuba and Mexico are officially friends. It would annoy the Mexicans if they found Cuba selling wea-pons to their rebels. What about the money?"

"We didn't find it."

"Okay, where's the launcher?"

"Why couldn't you shut Avila down?"

"We were going to catch them all with dirty hands," Nash said. "But that piss-ant mayor of yours decided to go big time. He and *her* old man intercepted the fucking thing."

"Took the money and lived happily ever after?" Bar-ry said.

"Ask Yates about that. I notice you didn't find any ID for Daniel Trevor." He unfolded his arms. "If you've got a Stinger, we want to see it."

"No reason you shouldn't," said Deputy Chief Pohl from the wall. "Joint recovery, joint credit on the busts, if any."

Nash shrugged.

"And we prosecute Avila for homicide," Pohl said.

"You know he's going to end up in federal hands," White said. "There's nothing Randy and I can do about that."

"We'll talk about it," Pohl said.

White nodded. "Irv, give me an estimate on how many launchers you've got?"

"Judging by the crates?"

"Sure."

"Three dozen."

White looked stunned. "Are you sure?"

"Does it matter?"

"They go for a half-million each." He blew silently.

Nash looked at me. "Makes you wonder, doesn't it? Who was the last fucker standing on that boat?"

I tried to ignore him, but couldn't.

"Let's go see what you've got," White said.

Hobbes's boat sat at a far slip screened from the road by a houseboat. Lights were on in the marina office and in a few of the live-aboards. Seeing us on the catwalk, Hobbes lowered his shotgun and stepped out of the boat onto the planks.

"You gonna let the feds screw it up?" he said.

"Uh-huh," said Barry, and introduced them.

They went aboard while I stayed on the walkway. There was less excitement in town tonight. Not having captured Avila, the agencies seeking him assumed he had escaped the island.

Across the water, a radio came on in a neighbor's sailboat, and the familiar cadence of the BBC report filled the marina. The sailboat's owner, Toby Gould, refused to wear a hearing aid. I looked at my watch. Past nine p.m.

My phone rang and Gloria Hutchin sounded concerned. "Are you all right, dear?"

"I'm fine."

"I still have contacts in the Cuban community and I don't like what I'm hearing. Avila is looking for you, Megan. Would you like to spend the night with me? A few of my boys are here. We'll have too much music, much too much false cheer, and you'll be safe."

There was less risk of an entanglement I didn't want at Gloria's than at Barry's apartment. But I planned to be up bright and early for the trip to the *Two Earls*. The recovery would begin in earnest tomorrow.

"I think I've got myself covered, but thank you."

"There's another reason. My Cubans think they know what happened to Hubbard."

My mouth was dry. "Tell me."

"Not on the telephone. Come over. We'll have a drink. I'll tell you what I know."

Nash and White were coming off Hobbes's boat, the younger man carrying a missile tube on his shoulder. He wore the smile of a kid who planned to shoot something down.

38

Every light in Gloria Hutchin's house seemed to be on. Pineapple-shaped cutouts glowed on the shutters, and torch light from the garden slipped past the branches of banyan and joewood trees. A young man in red bikini pants met me at the side gate and ran ahead to the swimming pool. He jumped from the chill air into the steaming water where Gloria was frog-kicking beneath the surface. She wore a gold tank suit that made her as sleek as a sixteen-year-old.

She climbed out and pulled on a robe. In the reflected light, her brown face was withered, her limbs were shrunken muscle and sinew. Her thighs bore shore white scars. She shooed away a boy who brought us drinks.

"I really don't like Cubans," she said. "They kept

me eight years before I was traded. The worst prison was on that filthy island. Now it's the Isle of Youth, and tourists go to the beaches."

She stared at me with something like pity, suspecting that I couldn't survive all that she had survived. Music jolted on, and lights flashed rhythmically in one of the small houses at the back of her compound. Gloria raised her voice. "I couldn't remain gloomy, dear. My boys reminded me I had promised them a party."

A rumba pounded from the speakers around the garden. A dark man in a thong moved around the pool swinging an incenser. Gloria sipped her drink.

"What have you done to make Avila hate you?" she asked.

I told her most of the ruse.

"So he looks foolish," she said. "That's reason enough to kill you. Cubans make Sicilians look forgiving and tender."

"I'll be careful."

"I hope so." She gave me a sad look that I understood wasn't only for myself. "I asked a few old friends about Hubbard. Word that I was interested got around in the resistance groups. To some of them, Tia Gloria is a hero. One of the men who tortured me lives in Largo. Poor sadistic pig is so contrite he would wash my feet if I let him. He believes Hubbard is dead. It seems Avila dumped the body of an Anglo out in the straits a few days ago. It may not be true."

I nodded.

"I'm sorry it's bad news. My friends say Hectorcito is no longer trusted by the people from Havana. They're not certain he didn't steal their money." Lifting her glass, she said, "Fuck them all."

"The long and the short and the tall?"

She smiled. "I'm freezing. Why don't you stay the night? The boys will subside by midnight. You look much worse for wear. Have you heard from that artist lout? I'm not certain this is a secret, but those two he went off with smuggle pot. Should we hope your friend doesn't get caught at that?"

Trying to picture Tim, I conjured up an empty blond oval instead of a face. I remembered pale hands that were not strong. The speed with which he was vanishing should tell me something—perhaps that I should go to bed only with guys who had strong hands.

"You're barely on your feet," Gloria said.

I nodded. "My mind is in worse shape." I told her my silly conclusion about men's hands and she laughed.

"Listen, dear. It's as good a rule as any. I used to prefer men with mustaches, until I got to know so many of them."

I had never seen much of her main house. Like a lot of people in the tropics, Gloria lived and entertained on porches and patios. The first level of the house, where I'd been before, was open and uncluttered. A polished plank floor stretched from the back door to the front wall, broken only by Kabu rugs and a couple of tall plants. A stairway rose to a railed bal-cony that showed several doors to other rooms.

"There's a room with its own bath you can use," Gloria said. "I'm going to have a shower and crawl into bed. Tomorrow we'll have breakfast."

"I have to get started early," I said.

"Then tiptoe out, and we'll have dinner. Aunt Gloria intends to sleep late. Do you need one of my boys to take you somewhere?"

"It's only to the marina, and I still have Hub's car."

"If you change your mind, feel free to wake any of them. Aunt Gloria's boys need to earn their keep."

The bed was a small four-poster with a carved headboard and a hooked spread. The room's white-washed walls were empty except for a sepia-toned print of an old waterfront scene that hung beside the door. I hooked my knapsack on a bedpost, shed my clothes in a heap on the floor.

The deep rump-rump of music vibrated in the bones of the house. I was too tired to care.

39

No nightmares, no screaming. It was still dark. I was awake for another reason.

The stillness in the house was deep and complete, as if it hadn't been disturbed for quite a while. I glanced at my watch.

3.28 a.m.

I closed my eyes, willing sleep.

But there was too much to think about. In an hour and a half, Ellsworth Hobbes would take his boat out to our spot on the Gulf. I wanted to be on board. This time we would be joined by a flotilla of official vessels, whose men and women would take over the investigation. Whether they would find my father's bones down there mattered to me more than any inventory of weapons.

Swinging my feet off the bed, I groped around for my clothes, pulled things on in the dark.

There was a light in Gloria's room, which was the next one along the balcony. I stepped past the open door, then stayed to look. The layout was almost identical to the other bedroom except the four-poster was larger and the bedspread and lampshades were pale yellow. The bed was neatly made. From the threshold I could see that the bathroom was dark. I crossed the balcony, found a light switch and went downstairs.

In the kitchen an open container of yogurt and a saucer of blueberries sat next to the sink. The pool lights were off, the torches quenched, the garden and cottages dark—except for the building on the right, a tiny, story-and-a-half house built in what they call cracker style, low on the ground, a little front porch, sloping tin roof. Lights shone on both levels.

She had gone looking for company among her free-loaders, I supposed, leaving alone the freeloader who slept nearest her and looked worse for wear. That made her kinder than most people would have been if they needed a companion in the wee hours. She had let me sleep.

There is a distinctive silence in the Keys before anyone starts thinking about dawn. No airplanes, sometimes no street traffic, televisions gone mute and blind, no breeze, no arguments, no saloon music if you're lucky enough to be away from the saloons. The silence adds up to a sense of exaggerated distance, as if the miles separating this place from Miami or Tampa are too great to cross.

I walked down to the cottage.

She stood in the lighted doorway. Speaking to someone inside the cottage, she hadn't heard me approach. She looked around.

"Oh, dear."

"I couldn't sleep either," I said.

"Well, good morning."

Stepping aside, she made a little gesture that I could go in ahead of her. I did, and there was a flutter of movement behind the door. A small muscular man was there, holding a knife. I moved before taking in more than that, and the knife flashed past my side. He landed on the wrong foot, which let me widen the distance between us in the small room.

Then I faced him. Pinky.

"I didn't want you hurt," Gloria said. Her voice was convincingly sad. She looked sideways at Pinky. "Don't prolong this."

He rushed and I got an easy chair between us. Doing so put my back in a corner. He feinted left, then right. Raising the knife, he flicked it back and forth letting me admire the double-edged blade. Then he climbed onto the cushioned seat of the chair. As I crouched, I reached behind me. I swung the automatic in line with his face and squeezed the trigger.

The hammer snicked. He moved in.

"No, wait," Gloria said as I scrambled along the wall. "Megan, dear, it doesn't have to be painful."

Coming toward me, she had a hand outstretched. "You should have woken long after they were gone. This makes me *so* unhappy."

I pointed the empty gun at her.

"Come, dear. I have some pentothal. It will be like going to sleep." The old mouth tried to smile. "Better than the knife, don't you think?"

Did she really think I would come to her? Against my will I did, a step. A drug was definitely better than the knife.

Pinky was ready in case I changed my mind.

"I'm sorry, Megan."

A second step, close enough. On the third step, I broke her knee.

Her leg bent the wrong way and she screamed as the knife jabbed my knapsack. The thrust helped me toward the door.

After the brightness of the room, the garden was impenetrably dark. Right away I stumbled on a raised brick and felt Pinky stabbing the air inches behind me. I pitched sideways, trying to avoid a tree, ran a few more steps. A faint reflection of the sky on water kept me from plunging into the pool. I tried to run left and bumped into a torch, which flexed and came loose. I held on for balance. I'd lost track of him.

He was silent. No muttered *putas*, no threats.

When I saw a sparkle of light on the blade, it was almost too late. He was a half-dozen feet away. I lifted the bamboo torch pole, jabbed hard. He *oofed* as the spiked end went into him. I threw my weight

223

forward, drove him back several steps.

In the dark he groaned. I couldn't tell how near he was as I crouched beside the pool and groped through my knapsack. The spare magazine held bullets. My fingers felt the cratered hollow point ends. I loaded the gun, went back to the little house.

Gloria was on her back, an arm across her eyes. Hearing footsteps, she struggled up, grimacing in pain, then subsided when she saw who had returned.

Eyes closing, she said, "Silly little bitch."

I slammed the door.

"Do you remember," she said in a reflective tone, "that dumpy red-diaper girl Tania? The one who ran with Che Guevara?"

"Never heard of her."

"She believed Gloria was her friend, her big sister who loved all the same ideals. The simple-minded creature couldn't imagine a friend betraying her. I wasn't much older than you, Megan, living in Havana in deep cover, betraying them all."

"Did you murder Tania?" I said.

"I suppose I helped. I knew where she and Che were operating in Bolivia. They were recruiting pea-sants to spread the revolution. The army ambushed them. Never mind. Just an old woman reminiscing."

An old centipede, I thought, exposing its black soul. Or pretending to. I was alert to the door, the window, the stairway.

"Is he here?"

"Who, dear?"

"Avila."

The smile must have cost her a lot. I watched the stairs.

"He doesn't stay here, for God's sake. He's a psychopath, a liability to everyone. Julian always said he would be a problem."

The Cuban diplomat on the sunken Hatteras was Julian Torres. I wondered if that was who she meant, but I didn't care enough to ask.

She gasped in pain. Shock was wearing off. "Don't judge me too harshly, dear. I'm a woman alone. We have to make our way in the world."

"What was Pinky doing?"

She closed her eyes, didn't answer.

"Gloria."

"I asked Hector to send him. I lacked the heart to take care of everything tonight."

"Like me."

"You were supposed to live, Megan. Pinky had another task. Did you actually manage to kill him?" When I didn't respond, she grimaced. "Do you mind calling an ambulance, dear? You hurt my leg badly."

I stood up. "Maybe they'll amputate it," I said, lifting the gun to point at the top of the stairs where I heard movement.

They came into view together, a svelte man in a blue-flowered yukata whose shoulder supported the diminished weight of the bigger man. They tottered and recovered, but the bigger man had trouble again with his legs. The slender man was Asian, I couldn't define it any closer than that, with thrusting cheek-bones and pretty amber eyes. Clearly he was strong. Hubbard Bennell, whom he supported, was slack-skinned and trembling. Hub dragged a hand across his ruined mouth and said something to the other man, who lowered him to sit. All I could hear was his leaky-pipe breathing.

The Asian man came down the stairs quickly, glanced at the old woman and slipped out the door.

I went up the stairs to Hub. His fingers were crusted with blood. His feet looked boiled. He wore sagging bloody underpants. The wall supported him.

"She's a monster," he snuffled, as if it were a secret between us.

Gloria had her eyes open.

"She tortured me. *He* said it didn't matter anymore; *he* believed me. But she kept on."

"Avila believed you."

He nodded. "I didn't know squat."

I thought of telling him he should be glad she hadn't lost interest, that absorbing pain had kept him alive.

"Is Avila here?" I said. I tried to watch two directions, especially the dark rooms above me, as he trembled.

"I sure hope not," he whispered. Then he got a moment's self-control. "I think they're all gone but her." He pressed both fists under his nose. "Stay away from her. She'll hurt you."

She was watching us, that was all.

"No, she won't," I said.

40

The paramedics wanted to give the nice old woman their first attention. I told them she was in my custody and they were needed upstairs. A few minutes later the police arrived and found an impaled man crying in the garden. More lights came on. We were a noisy party. Young men stuck their heads from the doorway of the neighboring cottage.

Terrence and an older cop stood near Gloria's stretcher. Barry put a finger on the younger man's chest. "Stick with her. Until a female officer shows up, you're with the old bag when she uses a bedpan. Got it?"

"Yes sir," said Terrence.

Barry leaned over Gloria. "Do you feel like talking?"

"I don't believe so."

"Where is Avila?"

"Silly Hectorcito."

"If he kills someone else, I'm going to charge you as an accessory," Barry said.

Despite her pain she moued. "I'm seventy-three, Mr. Policeman. Do you think an extra charge will matter?" She shifted on the stretcher, trying for a comfortable position. "Where's the morphine? I'm injured. I'm entitled to morphine." She looked up at Barry. "Besides, you stupid shit, twelve months from now I'll be in witness protection. All your little charges will go away."

I followed Barry outside. Pinky was alive but in no shape to be questioned. We moved on to the street. Barry phoned Ellsworth Hobbes a second time and warned him again to be alert for strangers.

He put away the phone. I went to the ambulance where Hubbard Bennell lay sobbing.

"You'll be okay," I said.

He shook his head, denying the possibility. They loaded him and closed the doors.

Barry was scanning faces. Not much of a crowd had formed. There weren't any saloons for blocks, just private homes and guest houses. A few people had come out onto porches.

"Avila hasn't got a chance of getting to the *Two Earls*," Barry said. "So his entire operation is a write-off." He gave the street a final sweep. "Gloria is probably telling the truth on one thing. Avila would like to kill you."

He was a natural at it, so I didn't scoff.

We picked up sandwiches and orange juice at a diner and cut across the island to the marina, where Ellsworth Hobbes was on the unlighted deck of his boat doing stretching exercises.

"Any sign of Nash?" Barry said. It wasn't quite dawn.

"Early yet. Don't trip on the shotgun."

Stepping onto the deck, Barry offered Hobbes a sandwich and a bottle of juice. They sat on a bench, leaning against a box of life vests.

"Thought you might have left during the night to see if the money was still there," Barry said.

"How much money?"

"Could be fifteen million, give or take a few. That's what ATF says the toys would be worth."

"Lot of money if it's still there." Hobbes looked at the chunky watch on his wrist. "We could have an hour's jump on everyone. Do we have to share with *her*?"

Barry looked at me. I said: "Do we have to share with *him*?"

"Already we're planning to kill each other," Hobbes said.

"Probably the money's not there."

"So there's no need."

"We'd probably have to kill Nash and White, too," Barry said. "They know we know."

"I knew there'd be a plus if we talked it out,"

Hobbes said. He chewed his sandwich. "So why are we sitting here?"

"Your boat."

"You sure we get to kill those two dorks?"

"If we want to keep the money. We might be able to buy off White; he's got some years in. But Nash is gung-ho. So we'd have to do them both." Barry was looking at the stars.

"I shoot 'em, you weight the bodies down."

"S*he'll* want dibs on Nash."

Hobbes seemed to think about it. Finally, he said, "Okay."

I was sitting on top of the life vest box, higher than the men, so I was first to see the headlights come into the yard.

"Now's your chance," I told them.

Nash and White climbed out of the light-colored Bronco near the office and came down the walkway. Barry got up and waved to them, stepping in front of me. He stumbled at the same moment I heard the wood-splitting *thwack*. He jerked as a second slug hit him. As he collapsed, something hummed past my face. Another crack. Rolling off the box, I saw Hobbes kneeing across the deck, caught a glimpse of Nash with his gun out.

I rounded the bench on my belly. I hadn't drawn my gun. There were enough of those pointing across the quiet marina, not finding a thing. The *thwacks* had been from one or more rifles. Very distinctive. There wasn't going to be a target within range of my handgun. Hobbes leaned on one knee, his shotgun probing the darkness.

It was very quiet.

Nash dropped into a crouch. He was too exposed to bother running for cover. I couldn't see his partner. Hobbes was barely disturbing the silence with a stream of curses that someone a few feet away could have mistaken for prayers.

Barry wasn't moving. I tried finding a pulse. The hole in his chest bubbled red. He groaned, and the blood came faster. It splashed the deck, ran past my feet, swirled into the scuppers. As I tried to plug the wound with scraps from my shirt, Ellsworth cried into a phone for help.

41

My boyfriend Tim came back from Belize on the twenty-fourth day of January. I drove a borrowed car to the Key West International Airport, watched the tall, ponytailed man hurry down the steps of the commuter plane from Miami.

"You wouldn't believe the rain down there," he said. "The whole country is a mosquito pond."

Three weeks hadn't changed him, but it let me see him with clear eyes. He expected me to forget that he had ditched me because our relationship crippled the artist within. Driving to the airport, I had been afraid my anger would melt on the first hug. He grabbed my shoulders and gave me a hot on-the-lips kiss. He thought the pain he had caused me didn't count. We would take up where we had left off.

"Where are Kevin and Grace?" I asked.

"You won't believe it. They got busted for trafficking. Some DEA types came with the local cops."

"What about you?"

"They didn't care about the rest of us. Just gave us back our passports and said git." He hunched under two duffel bags and held a small knapsack by a strap. His arms were pale and thin, his face the fair kind that never took a tan so he had to keep out of the sun. In a few years the gingery hair would be letting scalp show through. Then the whole getup, the embroidered jeans and collarless shirt and beads at his hairy throat, would be absurd.

I carried his knapsack as we headed for the car.

"It's good to be home," he said. "That was a weird scene down there. Nobody doing dick, just getting wrecked. I shouldn't have left you."

I kept walking.

"I spent the money I had," he said. "Was planning to surprise you with that, maybe get something nice for the boat."

And mail it from Belize?

Without breaking stride, I gave him the news. "You can't move back aboard."

He stopped. I kept walking.

"Why not?" he called.

If I told him all the reasons—even the little one, that it's hard to get back in bed with a guy you're starting to see as absurd—he just wouldn't get it. I kept it simple. "I'm not all that attracted to you anymore."

He looked scared. His voyage of self-discovery hadn't turned up much, I suspected, and he didn't want anyone to know.

"*Come on*, Megan."

That was what really ticked me off. No matter what illusions he had lost about himself, he was sure he was still okay for me. All he had to do was say, *Come on,* Megan.

"You really believe in kicking a guy when he's down," he said. "I thought I'd been doing enough kicking for both of us. But you wouldn't know about that, would you?"

"I'll drop you downtown," I said. "Piers-Paul is supposed to be looking for a roomie."

Tim settled in the car before he thought to ask. "Who's ride is this?"

"A friend's."

He looked at the beaten-up seats with the dawning thought that maybe the problem wasn't him, the problem was that I could be had for an old car. I broke the speed limit getting Tim into town.

Barry Irvington demanded the day's news and was annoyed when I had nothing. No Avila sightings. Nobody shooting at me. He knew everything I knew about the *Two Earls* and probably more. No significant amount of money had been found by the government's divers. In a stateroom they had discovered a skull with two bullet holes and other bones that yielded DNA matching Cole Yates's. Several questions answered, several not. Unsatisfactory, in the view of my hospitalized friend.

I arrived at six-thirty as usual, when he was done with dinner but before he got sleepy. Tonight Randy Nash was leaving. He grinned and punched me in the shoulder.

"He likes you," Barry said when the agent was gone. "Ever since he found out you fight dirty, he's been walking around with music in his head."

Imagining Nash with music in his head was more than I could do without shivering. I looked around the hospital room. It was tidy, and I had an unpleasant suspicion why hospitals keep things that way. Cleaning up after a packrat like me had died could take days.

"Is there anything I can get you?" I said.

"The nurses take good care, you don't have to." He had been out of bed off and on for three days, out of ICU several days before that. He showed no sign of dying, but he looked sunken as he sat in his striped pajamas and bathrobe, and much older. The wounds were healing and the pneumonia had been quelled, and he expected to go home in a few days and back to work in a couple of months. Ridiculed by Ellsworth Hobbes for not taking full disability, he had given a feeble shrug. He was afraid to retire. Treasure diving was too dangerous.

"So you have nothing to report," he said.

"No."

"Well, Nash had. The pathologists digested the bones we sent them. None of them matches your father's Xrays or DNA."

I wandered around the room, wondering what I should think about those facts.

"It doesn't mean Dan didn't sink Avila's boat and get himself killed," Barry said, as if he were closing a door I wanted to leave open.

"It doesn't mean anything one way or the other."

That didn't satisfy him. "A body outside the boat could have been carried for miles, bones scattered like twigs. You should let it go."

I hadn't dreamt for days about the faceless things in the water. There was no reason not to let it go.

No reason, if I didn't count a sense of loss that felt like betrayal. I had caught myself thinking the lying bastard had better be dead. I didn't know what he had done, or for whom. I was going to bed angry and waking up angry. Even Lem Rees at the Carbuncle commented disapprovingly on my lousy mood.

"You know," Barry said, "when my wife took off, I was sore for months that I hadn't gotten a chance to say don't let the door hit you. You're in sort of that position."

"I'm not in a mood for psychological counseling."

"No, I can tell. There's leftover coleslaw on the night stand. Would you like some?"

"I would rather eat chili at the Carbuncle."

He nodded. "If your pilot friend is buying, I'm sure you would."

I didn't answer. The healthier he felt, the more he commented on my life. I had gone dancing and drinking with Steve Taylor exactly twice in the last ten days. How it was going to work out I wasn't sure. Not quickly, it seemed. But I had flown out to the Tortugas with him four times, and after the last flight he told me how well I'd kept unruly teenagers in line. He meant it as a compliment, but it annoyed me. Was that the best he could think of?

"So what ails you?" Barry said. "You don't feel guilty about the Hutchin woman?"

"No." I thought about it, made sure. "No. She was talking about some girl she had betrayed, it must have been forty-five years ago. Tania. Should I know the name?"

"Gloria had been at the game a long time. There would have been a lot of betrayals. I don't know the name Tania." He leaned back. "You know better than to feel guilty about me."

"Sure," I said, not meaning it.

"You're keeping your head down?"

I wanted to ask him how careful I could be and still step outdoors. If Avila wanted me badly enough, he would try again. I hoped none of my other friends got in the way.

When Barry said he wanted to go to sleep, I flicked off the lights and left. I skulked down the hall feeling grateful that he was alive, a little exposed that he knew too much about me. But there weren't that many people who did, it wasn't as though they formed a crowd. At most a small club, made up of people who needed a laugh now and then.

I drove out to the air charter office. Steve was closing up. The hard evening light put burnt orange edges on all the angles of his body. He was leaning over the desk like some Wild West cowboy from the days when the movies made them all clean-shaven and well-scrubbed, hetero and polite. He was too square by half, not a tattoo to be found, but I guessed I could get used to that.

"You look like you're thinking about something," he said.

I was always thinking about something. But I shook my head. I didn't want to talk about Danny Trevor tonight.

"My bank account's flush," I said. "I'll buy you dinner at Louie's."

We would go top of the line.

"You're awfully generous tonight," he said, smiling as if he wondered what else I had in mind. Rather than ask, he would wait and see.

A nice guy. I needed one of those.

3315119

Made in the USA